Feeling his hand on her, she felt sexy and so close to him. For the first time, she wanted to kiss him and wondered what it would feel like if they made love, not just sex for a quick fix until the next time she needed it, but really make love, feeling the passion in every fiber of her body. After she told him the truth about her past life, would he ever want to see her again? He treated her gently, like a precious flower. She wouldn't be the decent woman and fifth-grade teacher that he saw now. Maybe he was too good for her, and to think that he wanted the schoolteacher and precious flower made her heart ache. Lord, she thought. What woman could resist him?

After Autumn and Philip walked around the grounds, she was proud to introduce him to her peers. At 1:00 PM, they left.

"What do you have planned for the rest of today?" Philip asked.

"I hadn't made any plans. But I do need to go to my apartment to make a couple of phone calls. Why don't we have lunch?"

"I was hoping that you would ask. Do we need to stop and buy anything?" He couldn't stop himself and gave her another quick kiss on her cheek.

Autumn smiled and grabbed his hand to lead him to their cars. "How about pizza?"

"And beer?" he asked.

"And beer," she replied and laughed. That was another thing she loved about him. He made her laugh so easily. "There is a Shaky's Pizza on the way."

Philip walked Autumn to her car. She was wearing a red sweater that emphasized her perfectly sized breasts. The jeans were tight across her hips, and she had a sexy walk that made him want to watch her all day. He shook his head to calm the excitement in his mind, but what man didn't want to be in love with a woman that aroused him every time he thought of her?

Also by Patricia Ann Phillips

NO TURNING BACK

LAST BRIDE STANDING

NICE WIVES FINISH FIRST

JUNE IN WINTER

Published by Kensington Publishing Corp.

BACK TO
BASICS

PATRICIA ANNE
PHILLIPS

Kensington Publishing Corp.
http://www.kensingtonbooks.com

DAFINA BOOKS are published by

Kensington Publishing Corp.
850 Third Avenue
New York, NY 10022

All Kensington titles, imprints, and distributed lines are available at special quantity discounts for bulk purchases for sales promotions, premiums, fund-raising, and educational or institutional use. Special book excerpts or customized printings can also be created to fit specific needs. For details, write or phone the office of the Kensington special sales manager: Kensington Publishing Corp., 850 Third Avenue, New York, NY 10022, attn: Special Sales Department, Phone: 1-800-221-2647.

Dafina and the Dafina logo Reg. U.S. Pat. & TM Off.

ISBN-13: 978-0-7582-2384-5
ISBN-10: 0-7582-2384-6

First mass market printing: April 2009

10 9 8 7 6 5 4 3 2 1

Printed in the United States of America

Acknowledgments

To my son Darren, and my daughter, Cassandra.
You are the light of my heart.
Thank you to my mother for always being there.
Thanks to all my sisters and brothers
for the laughter and good times we have together.

To Rakia Clark, thank you for being my editor.
It's really nice working with you.

A special thanks to the book clubs and the fans
that continue to read my books.

Chapter 1

After applying red lipstick over her full lips, foundation over her face, and black eyeliner, Autumn Evans stood in front of the mirror to see if she looked like herself, or masqueraded as someone else. She made up her face to look different; it made it easier to become someone else instead of herself. She did not look like the teacher of fifth-grade students. It was like a game she played that was repeated day after day.

She opened the dresser drawer and pulled out a condom, then stared at herself in the mirror trying to make excuses for the reason she was going out again. She felt ill as she thought of her life, and the lie that she had been living. Thinking about it only made it worse, but it still made her realize right from wrong. And what she did was wrong; dangerously wrong, enough to ruin her life forever. The life she lived was spinning out of control as the nights grew dark beyond darkness and the days more gray than the day before.

Autumn pushed the condom inside her purse, strutted to the living room and out the door. She drove off without giving her behavior another thought.

Autumn was a fifth-grade schoolteacher and was loved by all the children. She was a member of the PTA and worked alongside the principal to make a difference for the children in Compton, California. She was nominated twice for teacher of the year, and every child wanted to be in her classroom. Autumn was soft-spoken, she wore small black-framed glasses, and her black hair hung to her shoulders. The thought of losing her career because of her behavior made her ill.

Autumn parked her car in front of a small bar on the corner of Grand Avenue in El Segundo, California. She ambled inside the bar, adjusted her eyes to the darkness, and headed for the bar. Autumn knew it would take only minutes before a gentleman would send her a drink, and as always, a drink was sent to her before she finished the first one she'd ordered. She spotted a tall gentleman and swirled around on the barstool to give him a dazzling smile.

The man was sitting alone in the corner. He got up and asked Autumn to join him, and she accepted. She took full measure of him as he pulled a chair out for her. He was handsome enough; the scent of his cologne was stimulating. He also looked as though he was married—the well-kept type—not that it made any difference to her. She would be with him only one night. Funny how she had learned to tell the married from the single ones, and the single from the gay ones.

"What's your name, honey?" the man asked.

"Mary Kay." Rule one, she never gave her real name, where she lived, or what she did for a living. No one needed to know.

"My name is Jerome." He smiled and noticed her sexy, full lips.

Autumn was sure Jerome wasn't his real name. He was out to get laid just as she was. After a short conversation, and knowing his purpose, she would perform her charade as always. After one drink, she picked up her purse and pretended that it was time for her to leave.

"You're leaving me so soon, Mary Kay? We haven't had time to get to know each other yet."

"Sorry, but I have a full day's work tomorrow. I have to get up at five in the morning." She smiled as she saw the need in his eyes. He wanted her.

"Come on, spend some time with me. I hate going home to a lonely, cold house," he pleaded. "I'll take you to a nice hotel, anything you want. I just don't want to go home now. You see, my mother is gravely ill and I had to get out of the house to clear my head. I can make you sleep like a baby when you get home."

She looked at his face and knew that he was lying, but so was she. Finally, she nodded with approval. "I don't usually do this the first night that I meet a man." Autumn always made the men think her sleeping with them was their idea, and they treated her as though they were the luckiest men alive.

Autumn followed Jerome in her car. He made a left into the parking lot of the Hilton Hotel. They got out of their cars and walked inside. She waited in the lobby while Jerome went to register, which took only ten minutes.

Once they were in the room, he kissed her tenderly. Jerome began to undress her with skilled, fast hands, and Autumn lay on her back, brown thighs slightly parted. She watched him as he finished undressing himself and lay next to her. His body was long, dark, and well built. His face was young; he was maybe even five years younger than she.

"Do you want me? Do you want me?" she insisted. She had to hear it, and she had to know that he wanted her even more than she wanted him. Hearing it was one more reason to have sex with him, because he wanted her, too.

"Baby, I want you, I want you."

She felt him touch her, heard his moans, as she purred like a cat. She wanted him, needed his touch, his kiss, and, finally, she needed the contact that she was seeking; she needed him to enter her. Autumn took all of him, and he satisfied her urgent need for sex, and fed the need that stayed inside her. Then she got on top so she could feel him even deeper, bigger. He sent her where she needed to be. She wanted to be satisfied beyond her dreams. They made love for hours before Autumn decided it was time to leave.

Autumn didn't mind staying out so late. She had made up her mind that she would stop living two lives and get help.

After she had finished dressing, he offered her his business card. "You may need me again, and I want to spend more time with you. Just call me anytime during the day, and I will meet you."

He gave her a wide, alluring smile that warmed her heart. She reached for the card with trembling hands, and pulled her eyes from his face. Maybe if she used it, she would no longer have to go to bars and pick up strange men. But once she stepped out of the room, she crumpled the card and dropped it in a wastepaper basket next to the door. She didn't want to remember him, and she didn't want to see him again.

She had to stop before it was too late.

* * *

"Good afternoon, Autumn. I tried to come and see you earlier, but I had a busy morning," Diane said.

Autumn was eating a salad she'd made for lunch. She was eating at her desk, and a Pepsi sat in front of her. "I've been busy, too, and Kenya had a crying fit because I gave her a C on her book report. She's used to getting As and Bs. I tried to explain it to her that she just made an A on the math test last Monday."

"She's a smart child."

"I know," Autumn said, wiping the corner of her left eye. "Has anyone in Dorsey's family called today? I didn't get much sleep last night after her sister said the cancer had spread through her body."

"Dorsey is the reason I came to see you. She died at five this morning. The staff is really going to miss her."

"What?" Autumn asked. "I can't believe that I just saw her three days ago and now she's gone." Autumn was holding her Pepsi and set it back on her desk. "I just can't believe it."

Unable to speak, Diane only nodded.

Autumn stood up and walked to the window. The children were playing on the bars, and Kenya was laughing. She seemed to have gotten over the C on her book report. Funny how children cry about one thing, and fifteen minutes later they've gone on to something different.

"Did you know that we were the same age?" Diane asked.

Autumn took her seat again. "Yes, I knew."

Diane looked at her watch. "Lunch will be over soon. I just wanted you to know."

"Thanks." Autumn took a deep breath and watched

Diane as she walked out the door. She and Dorsey had been so close. As Autumn placed her hands against her face, Dorsey's death hit her in the pit of her stomach.

Autumn stepped inside her apartment, undressed, and went to the shower. Once she finished, she filled a glass with white wine and relaxed on the sofa.

She called Matthew, but he said that he was busy and would call her later if it wasn't too late when he got off duty. She slammed the phone down hard and was sorry before it hit the cradle. Matthew was a doctor, after all, and had lives to save. She had no right to be angry.

Autumn got up and refilled her glass with wine. Maybe if she drank enough, she would stay home and fall asleep. But the urges were taking over her mind and body. The sexual compulsiveness was intoxicating. The need for sexual contact was stronger than ever before, and the wine was causing her to feel light-headed. She should have known better than to drink on an empty stomach. The wine had gone to her head, and the urges were ruling her body and taking control of her mind. There wasn't anything she could do to stop it. Dorsey's death had taken a toll on her. By seven-thirty, Autumn was slipping into a tight pair of jeans and strutting fast out the door.

The quiet gentleman observed Autumn sitting at the bar ,with a martini on the counter in front of her and a man that seemed to be annoying her. He was vociferous and had no respect for women.

"If you didn't want to be picked up, then why would

you come into a bar, and why accept my drink?" he asked. He was glaring dangerously.

Autumn realized that she had made a mistake by accepting his drink or talking to him in the first place. He was beginning to frighten her, and as she held the glass, she had to force her fingers to stop quivering. She felt relieved to see the tall gentleman approaching.

"The lady was waiting for me. We had planned to meet here."

Autumn looked up at his face, and he winked and smiled down at her.

"Why didn't you say that you were here to meet someone, woman? You need to lay off the alcohol," he said as he pushed his empty glass across the bar and stormed out the door.

"Thanks. I was beginning to think that I was in trouble," Autumn said.

"You were getting there. What are you doing out here alone anyway?"

"Venting. I lost someone that I care about. Since I have to drive home, I better ease up on the drinking, like the man said."

"That's very wise." ·

She knew that she should go home, but she hadn't gotten what she needed, and she enjoyed looking at the hunk who stood in front of her. She took pleasure in his company, the smell of his cologne, the sound of his deep voice, and the full, sexy lips.

He looked at her finger, but there were no rings. A woman so beautiful had to have a man in her life, even if she wasn't married. Her brown skin was clear, her almond-shaped eyes were brown, and she had a nice figure. So, why was she in a bar, and alone, he wondered.

"So, who are you going home to tonight?" Autumn asked playfully.

The man looked down at her and smiled. "No one. I live alone." He sat on the barstool next to her and ordered a glass of wine. "My name is Jeff, what's yours?"

"My name is . . . Sharon." She held out her hand, and he took it.

Even though she had had a little too much to drink, he sensed her hesitation when he asked her name. And he was sure that it wasn't Sharon. "Can you drive home?" he asked with concern.

"I think so. But I have to if I'm going to get there."

Now, what was he going to do about her? No way would he leave her here. He would feel horrible if he read in the newspaper that she was found dead. Any man who came here after he left would want her and try to take advantage of the opportunity. He had to send her home in a taxi. He looked into her eyes; they were sad. The saddest eyes he had ever seen. But she was a desirable woman.

Autumn edged on the barstool so she could get closer to him. He saw the deep V-shape in the front of her sweater and the top of her bursting brown, smooth breasts. Her full red lips were turned up into a soft lazy smile; she was seducing him, luring him like a magnet. And he had lost all will to refuse her. Jeff looked deeply into her eyes; Autumn knew exactly what she was doing.

Autumn knew that she had him and he wanted her as much as she needed him. After all, he was a man.

"You don't really want to go home?" he asked.

"I don't think so, though I should."

"I can't let you drive, but if you go with me I'll bring you back to your car."

"I can't stay out too late, I'm a working woman," she whispered as she moved even closer to him.

"I'm a working man, so I can't stay out too late either." He had intended to buy himself only one glass of wine and go home. He had worked late and was still tense, but he hadn't anticipated spending time with a strange woman. Jeff reached for her hand. "Shall we leave?"

"Yes." She followed him outside.

Jeff helped Autumn inside his black Lexus SUV. Even in the dark, it shined like new. As he drove, he smiled when he saw Autumn lay her head back on the seat and close her eyes. He talked to her to keep her awake. Fifteen minutes later, he was in the parking lot of the Marriott Hotel in Marina Del Rey.

The lobby was quiet, with a short line of people checking in. "Here, you have a seat and I'll check in," Jeff said and gave Autumn's hand a gentle squeeze.

She watched as he walked away. Maybe it was the wine, but she felt a hint of aloneness as he left her. Even when he was at the counter being waited on, she watched him. There was something quiet and calm about him. He had a handsome, chiseled face and a cleft chin. His broad shoulders appeared powerful and his legs were long.

Jeff was back and reached for her hand. He led her from the elevator to Room 206, holding the door open for her to walk inside.

Autumn was still a bit light-headed, the wine buzzing in her head. She felt warm and sexy. She kicked off her shoes, and pulled her sweater over her head.

Jeff couldn't pull his eyes away as she undressed. Her body was curvy and brown, her breasts were beautiful, and her red panties were lace. She pulled the covers back and lay on the bed, waiting patiently for him.

Autumn watched him as he pulled off his watch and placed it on the nightstand. He was well-built and well worth waiting for. As though he'd forgotten, he picked up his trousers and pulled a condom from his pocket. She was relieved that he used caution. She never had sex with any of the men without a condom.

He lay on the bed beside her and gathered her in his arms. "You don't have to do anything that you don't want to."

"I know."' She turned to face him, and he kissed her. Autumn gently whispered in his ear, "Do you want me, Jeff? Tell me now. Do you really want me?"

"I want you, baby. You know that I want you," he whispered softly, pulling her closer to him.

She gasped as his warm tongue circled the tip of her nipples. He raised her legs even higher, and she wrapped them around him. She wanted this man inside of her, deep, deep inside her. She wanted him over and over again. No, it was the wine. He could mean nothing more to her. And why would he want a woman who slept with a stranger? No, it was too much wine. The rule was never to see them again, never get attached or answer too many questions, and Jeff was no different.

"Do you love it, Sharon? Say it's good." He was deep inside her, then grabbed her hips and pulled her closer to him. "Do you love it, baby? Say it so I can hear."

"I love it, I love it. Now, now," she said in a rush. No one had ever handled her so gently, but held her firmly with deep strokes, making her feel every inch of him, and she wanted more. Her sweaty body arched up to him, taking all she needed.

After two orgasms, she forgot that she was with a stranger. It was as though they had known each other before. No man had ever taken her so expertly and made her want so much more. No man.

They made love for hours, and when he let her go, she fell into a deep slumber.

The next morning the sun streamed through the windows, waking her with a start. She opened one eye, feeling the sun glaring against her face, and the pain throbbed in her left temple. Then she slowly opened both eyes. The room was spinning as she looked around for anything familiar to help her remember the night before. Autumn sat up straight, her heartbeat quickening. Where was she, who had she been with? She could hardly remember his face. Finally, it started to float back. He was tall, nice, but she couldn't visualize his face and didn't remember his name. "My car?" she said out loud. "Did I drive my car?" She held both hands against her temples, trying to remember. Autumn got out of bed; she was naked. Then she saw a one-hundred-dollar bill and a note on the nightstand.

Left money for a taxi. Your car is parked in the parking lot at the Townhouse on La Tijera and Centinela. I had a wonderful time. Jeff. The note was impersonal, sweet and short, no last name, no phone number, and no I want to see you again. But wasn't that the way she always wanted it? He made sure that he didn't give her any unnecessary information about himself. *Who is he, and how will I know it's him if I see him again?* she thought. One hundred dollars; did he think she was a hooker? Of course he did. She felt tears on her cheeks and wiped them with the back of her hand. Another man, another hotel. It all had to end.

Autumn peeked out the window, then picked up a magazine. It was addressed to the Marriott in Marina Del Rey. Well, the man wasn't cheap. She could say that much for him.

It was six o' clock, and Autumn only had time to call a taxi, get her car, then go home to shower and get to school. But deep inside, she felt different than she had with the other men. She felt cheap, and the money he left only made her feel worse. If only she hadn't drunk so much, then she could remember his face.

Autumn was at school on time. The bell was ringing as she rushed inside her classroom. She placed her purse in her desk and went outside where the children were forming a line to go inside.

Autumn waited for the children, but her head felt as though it would explode, and she couldn't get the night before out of her mind. *Lord, help me stop this double life.* A teacher in the day, and a sex addict at night. Her life was a lie that she loathed.

Chapter 2

Autumn paced the floor as she waited nervously for Matthew. She looked at her watch; it was four-thirty. "He said that he would meet me at my apartment by five," she thought out loud. She heard the wind blowing and leaves sweeping into the streets as she stopped pacing and stood at the window, her forehead all but pressed against it, gazing, staring aimlessly into the streets.

Autumn folded her arms across her chest and closed her eyes, wondering why Matthew sounded angry on the phone. It had been a year since he'd gotten angry with her. They had always gotten along so well together and were complimented and envied by other couples who had gotten together the same time as she and Matthew and then gone their separate ways. Autumn and Matthew had dated for two years and would be married in four months. They had already planned their future together.

Autumn poured a glass of wine and sipped. God, she was becoming frigid as she waited for his arrival. She could hear her own heart beat, feel the hairs on her arms sticking up. Finally, the doorbell rang. Autumn took a deep breath, strutted to the door, and slung it open. Matthew walked past her; his hands were in his pockets as he turned to face her with an angry blur in his dark eyes that caused her to tremble with dread. Why did he look so angry?

Moments passed as he stared at her. She was dressed in a purple pantsuit. He assumed she had just arrived home from school before he got there.

Autumn placed her glass on the coffee table and took a seat on the sofa. Looking at Matthew's face made it impossible for her to stand any longer. Deep in her heart she knew what had happened. By the anger in his eyes she knew; he had found out about her double life, and she had tried to be so careful.

"*Where* were you last Tuesday night?"

"Matthew, that was a week ago. Let me think." Her mind was spinning fast. "Oh, Tonya and I were at the Beverly Center," she answered, but she could feel her throat going dry, and she reached for the glass of wine. "Possibly it wasn't Tuesday. I don't remember." She had lied to him, and she hated lying to Matthew. Their relationship deserved better. A relationship that she had always respected, always needed.

Matthew grabbed the glass from her hand. "Damn you. Don't tell me you can't remember where you were a week ago. Autumn, I ask you, where were you last Tuesday?" he asked between closed teeth. He was deeply hurt, and desperately needed to hear the truth from her.

Autumn had never seen him so angry. She felt cold and shivered, and swallowed hard before she could speak. "I think . . ."

Matthew kneeled forward, his face close to hers.

"You were in bed with a doctor with whom I practice. I showed him a photo of my fiancée and he recognized you. He told me about the night you two were together, and it was Tuesday night." Matthew grabbed Autumn's wrist. "He told me that I was going to marry a whore. The woman that I loved turns out to be nothing more than a whore. Was I not enough for you, Autumn? You have to pick up men in bars?" He released her and turned his back to her as though he could no longer tolerate her presence.

Autumn felt sick inside and leaped off the sofa standing behind Matthew. She tried to touch him, but couldn't. He knew now that she wasn't worthy of his love. Her double life was exposed.

"Matthew, you have always been enough for me. Don't you know how much I love you?"

"A year ago you cheated and said it was because we had separated for two months. I thought we were closer than ever. But you don't love me enough to be with only me. It's over between us. I can't marry you now. I would be the laughing stock at the hospital, and you will ruin my career. I want to be a great surgeon one day. I can't be that with a whore hanging on my arm." He started to the door and stopped, turned around to face her one last time when he heard her call his name.

"Please, don't let it end this way, honey. I'm dying inside, Matthew." She was sobbing, her hands reaching out to him. "Just let me explain what happened. I was in the bar with Tonya. When I was leaving, the man approached me. I don't know what happened or why I did it." She stopped, stumbled two steps backward when she felt Matthew's open hand against her face. The burning sensation caused her head to throb. Autumn was shocked and by looking at Matthew's face he was just as shocked as she was.

"I deserved that. I deserve whatever you do to me, but please don't leave me, Matthew. I can stop, and clean myself up. I know that I can stop," she pleaded through blinding sobs. Afraid he would walk out her door for the last time, she held on to his arm. "Please, we can get married and put this behind us. Give me one more chance, please." Her life depended on this moment, her future, the love for the only man that she wanted to spend the rest of her life with. "I can get help, baby," she whispered and placed her arms around his neck.

Matthew frowned in confusion as he listened to her. *What in hell is she talking about?* "Get help? All you had to do was be true to me as I've been to you. You're making no sense at all. I'm out of here, and I never want to look at your face again. Damn, why hadn't I seen you for what you really were? I don't know who you are." He pushed her aside and started to the door. But she wouldn't let go. She couldn't lose him.

"Please, help me, Matthew. I promise that I'll get help."

"Help to keep you from screwing every man that comes your way? Take your hands off me." He pushed her again and she fell against the wall, hitting the back of her head against a painting. But Autumn wouldn't give up. She knew that if Matthew walked out the door, he would never return. She was now facing the terror of her dreams—that Matthew would find out. Fear of abandonment and shame were the core of her addiction. Didn't he know that she was powerless over her sexual behavior?

Her head pounded like a drum. But she wouldn't let him give up on her, not now, not ever. She had to have Matthew. "You said you loved me. How can you just walk out and say it's over? I need a chance to try and help myself."

"What in hell are you talking about?" Even though he was angry and disgusted, he could see that she was desperate. "You want me to give you another chance to hurt and embarrass me? Is that what you are asking?"

"No. I need a chance for more counseling. Haven't you listened to anything I've been trying to tell you? I'm a sex addict. *A fucking sex addict.* I've been clean for over a year. I don't know what happened that night I slept with the doctor. But I can beat it again. I can do it if you help me, baby. I know that I can."

He needed the space and stepped back. No way would he let her touch him again.

Autumn saw his face stiffen; his eyes were as wild as an animal's. The hatred in them held her back. *Does he hear me? Does he even understand what I'm asking of him?*

"A sex addict? You've been sleeping around with different men all along, and I didn't know? How long? How many men have you slept with?"

His voice softened. She felt a glimmer of hope and took his hand, led him back to the sofa. She would spill her heart out to him. There would be no more secrets. No more double lives. Why hadn't she told him before? She closed her eyes and took a deep breath. Matthew was an understanding man. Surely he would empathize with her.

"When I was younger, I was sexually abused by

my uncle for two years. Later in life I became a sex addict. God, I hated him, and now I hate myself for hurting you. I hate myself for what I've become."

"Do you hate yourself more for hurting me or that I've found out what you are?" he asked bitterly, with a cold edge in his tone. She was not a woman he could continue to love, and as he looked at her his love for her was fading and being replaced with disgust and hatred. "I know what sex addiction is. I can't marry a woman who has the illness. You are not the Autumn I once knew and respected. What if you have AIDS? Oh, God, I could have AIDS, too." He placed both hands over his face and sighed deeply.

"I always made sure that a condom was used, and I was tested three months ago just to be certain that I'm safe, we're safe. I would never put your life at risk with AIDS or any other disease. I swear, baby." She saw his eyes resting on her with cold condemnation. Oh how he must hate her. "I don't understand you, Matthew."

"What's there not to understand?"

"You're a doctor. Surely you know that sex addiction is an illness. How can you walk out on me when I'm ill?"

"Easily. I don't trust you, and you didn't tell me. Someone else had to. Besides, I can't deal with it. It's damaging to my career, and who knows who may show up and say they slept with you? No, I can't deal with it."

Matthew stood up, and when Autumn started to stand, he held up one hand. "I know where the door is. I'm sorry, Autumn. Good luck."

"But, Matthew?"

He stopped at the door and turned to face her.

"We're finished. We're through. We're over." Matthew walked out the door, and out of her life.

Unable to speak, Autumn merely nodded. She knew there was no use running after him. It was over, and he hated her more than she hated herself. She held her head back and closed her eyes. Where would she go from here? A trail of tears fell from her eyes, but she couldn't move, she couldn't see anything but the hurt and shock in Matthew's eyes. She knew before he got to her apartment that he had found out about her unfaithfulness.

All of a sudden she felt as though her life were over. How would she get up tomorrow morning to go to work when there was no reason to? Her life had become empty, vacant, a hole in the middle of her heart.

After crying for hours, at ten that night Autumn finally forced herself off the sofa and slowly walked to her bedroom. She tried to sleep, but every time she closed her eyes she saw Matthew, heard his voice. *Whore, whore, whore,* was all she meant to him now. But to her, she was worse. As much as she loved teaching, at that moment it meant nothing to her. Everything that mattered was gone. She closed her eyes and prayed for sleep but to no avail. She got up and took a hot shower but it didn't relax her enough to help her fall asleep.

Autumn went to her closet and pulled out her jeans and a white blouse. She threw the blouse on her bed and pulled out a red sweater. "No, I can't do this," she yelled. Just once more. One more man, one more night of wild sex. Tomorrow will be another day. Tomorrow she would go back to rehab for help, and she would attend every meeting with the help of her family.

Tomorrow, her life would change, and she would become the woman she used to be before this terrible sickness took over her mind and body. Then she would go to Matthew and beg him, get on her knees if she had to. Autumn flopped down on the bed. Who was she kidding? Matthew would never take her back, she knew. He would never take her back.

Autumn brushed her hair back, applied some makeup, grabbed her purse, and rushed out the door.

She started to go to a bar in Westchester, California, but changed her mind. Besides, most men there already knew her. Instead, she went to a new bar that she had heard about in Inglewood, on Florence and Market Streets.

Autumn walked inside the bar and adjusted her eyes to the dim lighting. *Looks like tonight is my lucky night.* No waiting around for the right man to come along. There were five at a table and they watched her as she entered the door and walked over to the bar. She ordered rum and coke, and someone sent her a second drink.

"Who sent the drink to me?" Autumn asked the bartender.

"The second gentlemen at the corner table." He pointed in the direction of a table with three men.

Autumn turned around on the barstool as the tall man approached her. *Good,* she thought. He looked real good. All she wanted was to go to a motel, have a quick fix, and go home. Tomorrow she would phone in sick and ask Betty, her mother, to attend a meeting with her. Tomorrow couldn't come soon enough for her to go back to her old life again. But tonight, she needed the sex.

"Thanks for the drink." She admired his good-looking face and nicely built body. His shoulders were wide, and he was nicely dressed in all black, which gave him a handsome, dangerous appeal.

"My name is Zack. My friends and I couldn't keep our eyes off you. Are you meeting someone here?"

She saw him gazing at her full breasts. "My name is Mary Kay, and no, I'm not meeting anyone. I needed to go out for a while."

"I was hoping that we could talk and get to know each other better, and have a little fun. You see, I'm new in town, and it gets lonely when you don't have a pretty woman. After tonight, maybe we could become friends."

"What about your friends?" She sipped her rum and coke.

"I met them two weeks ago. We work together at the same place. And who cares, they can take care of themselves. I would rather be with you. What do you do for a living?"

"I work in a department store in Century City."

Zack saw her glance at her watch and pick her purse up off the bar. "It's a beautiful night. Why don't we go someplace so we can be alone? It's too noisy in here."

"Where would you like to go?" Autumn asked. He was easy. All men were so easy, she thought.

"We can go to a small motel around the corner. It looks like a nice, quiet place. You don't have a jealous husband to follow us, do you?"

"Of course not."

"I didn't think you did. But I had to ask. I would really like to know you, and treat you like a lady. Some time I would like to take you to dinner or a movie, and we can just hang out together, or do whatever you like. I'm an agreeable man."

She saw him smile as he looked at her face to see her reaction. But she had no intentions of ever seeing him again. He meant nothing to her.

"Like I said, I don't usually go with a man the first time we meet. But that smile of yours has won me over. You seem to be a good man that a girl can trust."

"That's me all right. I'll say goodnight to my friends and we can leave."

Autumn watched as he spoke with his friends. She thought of Matthew and started to jump off the barstool and run home, but Zack came back to get her. Maybe she should pass this one up, but she would never get any sleep or relaxation without the sex. And she needed a man so desperately. She would forget Matthew for thirty minutes. Thirty minutes was all she needed to help her through this night.

Autumn and Zack walked out. She followed him to a motel five minutes away. He got out first and went to her car. "You stay here and I'll come out to get you after I check in," Zack said.

"Okay. I'll wait," Autumn sighed. She wanted to go into the motel, then go right home. She was tired, and the thought of Matthew leaving her was overwhelming.

Five minutes and Zack was back. They went to Room 212 on the second floor at the end of the hall. After they got inside, Zack kicked off his shoes and so did Autumn. He gently took Autumn's hand and placed it against his lips, then led her to the bed. "Would you like to watch TV?"

"Yes, I guess so." She watched Zack as he grabbed the remote from the nightstand and flipped on the

TV, then took Autumn in his arms and kissed her tenderly. She admired him for his tenderness.

"I've wanted to kiss you since I first laid eyes on you. What did I do to get so lucky tonight?" He sat up and pulled off his white T-shirt, and began kissing her neck.

Autumn felt the familiar, warm stir inside and wanted his long, strong body bare and against hers. Zack seemed to be so gentle and nice to her. He undressed her down to her lace panties, and he finished disrobing.

Autumn watched him. It was thrilling to see him slowly pull his underwear down his long, strong, muscled legs. He was ready for her, and she felt fire and moist between her thighs. In seconds, Zack was on top of her. She felt as though she was in a unfathomable dream when she heard the soft knock on the door.

Zack held his head up. "I wonder who it is." he said. They heard a voice at the door.

"It's the manager. You forgot your wallet and I don't want to be responsible for what's inside of it."

Zack sighed. "What a jerk. I'll open the door slightly so he won't see you."

Autumn looked confused when Zack opened the door widely. She grabbed the sheet and pulled it up to her neck as Zack's friend from the bar stepped inside. "What does he want?" she asked, feeling fear build inside her. Leaving the bar with Zack wasn't such a good idea after all. She imagined that he was a freak and wanted someone to watch as he made love to her. She had to get out of there, but how?

"I want you. I thought old Zack might need some help. You see, Zack and I are brothers and what's good for one is good for the other." The man looked at her with a cold smile that caused a chill up her spine.

Autumn started to jump off the bed, but Zack jumped on top of her and held her down. "You're not going anywhere. We're going to have some fun with you, and make you love every minute of it. Aren't we, Danny?" he said, looking over his shoulder.

"Yes. This is the way we do it. What's good for Zack is good for his brother." Danny laughed and turned the TV up higher so no one could hear Autumn scream. They always screamed when he entered them from the back with his oversized penis. "Now, you seem like a nice little lady. Just do as we say and it's over. All three of us can have a good time."

"No. No." Autumn eyes were wide. She started to scream but Zack placed his hand over her mouth. "Shut the hell up. If you were home like the nice lady you pretend to be, you wouldn't have been the chosen one. We're here to give you what you want. You know it's what you want. Old Danny and I can't let you go home if you're not satisfied."

Autumn wanted to die before they killed her. She was sure that she wouldn't leave the motel alive. "Please, just let me go. No one will have to know anything about this. I just want to go home," she pleaded. She tried to get up again, but Zack pushed her down. "Please," she yelled, but before she could say another word, Zack placed one hand over her mouth. Her eyes were wide and tears rolled down the side of her face.

Zack entered her while Danny held her down. Autumn tried to fight, but to no avail. Danny grabbed a fistful of her hair and slapped her across her face. Blood gushed from her nose, and another punch in her left eye made her wish that she would die suddenly. The pain had become unendurable. Once Zack was finished with her, it was Danny's turn. He was rough, almost as though he hated her. He went deeply inside her, seemingly happy to hear her scream in pain. Autumn's hands were by her sides balled into small fists. She felt warm blood oozing from her nose and sliding down her throat. *God, please let me die,* she prayed to herself. Her left eye seem to hurt all the way to the back of her head, and her head felt too heavy to lift off the pillow.

When Danny exited her, Zack entered again. Autumn cried out loudly, and Danny punched her in her ribs. The sobs stuck in her throat, causing her to cough and choke. She could no longer see through her swollen eyes. She felt them position her on her back, her legs wide enough to cause more pain than she could bear as one plunged deeply inside her.

Autumn thought she had died and gone to hell. She had been punished for all her sins, but as she slowly lost consciousness she couldn't imagine hell being so cruel, or painful. She had been swallowed into hell. Her body was battered, her ribs were cracked, and her face was too bloody and swollen to recognize. Finally, she passed out and had no idea when they left her.

On their way out of the room, Zack opened Autumn's purse and pulled her wallet out. There was a neatly folded hundred-dollar bill. He took it out and dropped the wallet on the floor. He looked back at her and smiled. "She's sleeping peacefully, wouldn't you say Danny?"

"Yeah. Peacefully. Just like all the rest."

* * *

Autumn was in and out of consciousness when she heard voices around her. Her body felt as though it were broken in two when she was lifted off the bed. A police officer was asking questions that she was unable to answer. Then she could no longer see anyone around her, she could no longer hear the voices, or feel the movements, or see the light that made her eyes hurt so badly. Her body lay limp, still, as her mind floated from her.

Chapter 3

Lacy was the first family member to arrive at the hospital. She stood in the emergency waiting room, waiting for her parents to arrive. Calling them in the middle of the night to give them news of Autumn's critical condition was the hardest thing she'd had to do. She left her seven-year-old son home with her husband.

Lacy was sitting in a chair with her head back and her eyes closed when she heard the fast footsteps coming toward her. She knew that her mother would take charge and make a scheme.

"How is she?" Betty asked. Her breathing was labored, as though she'd been running. "Who would harm her, Lacy?"

"I don't know, Mom. I've been wondering the same thing. She's beaten up pretty badly." Lacy wondered why Autumn was out alone. What had really happened to her?

"Where is Matthew?"

"I don't know, Dad. I haven't called him yet."

"Well, call him, Lacy," Betty intervened. "You

should have called him as soon as you got here. Maybe he can tell us something, unless someone broke inside her apartment. I can't imagine Autumn being out so late without Matthew."

Lacy walked down the hall to a quiet spot with her cell phone in hand. She left her parents in the waiting room. Something was definitely wrong here. Why wasn't Autumn at home or with Matthew? It was three in the morning. The police officer said that she was found in a motel. What was she doing there? Lacy wondered. Lacy shook her head in confusion, but why so late, unless . . . unless she was forced? The thought turned her stomach. Someone had forced Autumn in a car and harmed her.

With regret, Lacy knew why Autumn was out so late. She hadn't gone to any of her meetings lately. But since she and Matthew were engaged, Autumn appeared to be so happy and content with her life. Everything seemed to be going so well. When did she start sleeping around again? Lacy certainly couldn't convey that information to her father. What father wanted to know that his daughter slept with strange men?

Lacy waited for Matthew to answer and blinked when she heard his voice. He sounded as though he had been sleeping.

"Matthew, Lacy here. Have you seen Autumn tonight?" She heard an impatient sigh into the phone.

"I saw her tonight when I broke our engagement. That was the last time I saw her. Why? Well, I suggest you go to the nearest bar, or maybe cruise down busy streets."

The phone clicked and Lacy held it in her hand for seconds before she pushed it inside her purse. "*Oh*

no, Autumn. What have you done?" Lacy went back
to where her parents were waiting. What could she
tell them? Goodness, all hell would break loose, and
what would her father say? What would the secrets
do to her parents trust in each other? From the beginning, Lacy was against keeping the secret from her
father. But no, Betty insisted that he not know. She
said that she would take care of everything. *Well,
mother dear, you can't fix this,* Lacy thought.

"Is Matthew coming?"

Lacy looked at Betty's eyes. It was time for all to
know. "No, Dad, Matthew isn't coming, and he and
Autumn aren't going to be married either."

Betty and Emmit looked at each other. "What was
going on, and if she wasn't with Matthew, then where
was Autumn when she was beaten?" Emmit asked,
standing up straight and tall.

Betty stared apprehensively at Lacy. She was sure
that Lacy would tell Emmit about Autumn's sex addiction. Just as Lacy started to answer, the doctor
came down the hall.

Lacy saw the relief in Betty's eyes, and turned to
face the doctor.

"Are you Miss Evans's family?"

"Yes, yes," Emmit answered. "How is my daughter?"

The doctor folded his arms in front of him and
leaned back on his heels. "She's in pretty bad shape.
Your daughter was terribly beaten, and roughly sexually abused. She's still not conscious, but I'm sure
she will be in a few hours. Whoever it was wanted
to see her hurt." He waited as Betty grabbed Emmit's
arm and stood closely beside him for support. The

doctor watched the couple as they held on to each other. Lacy wiped tears from her eyes.

"When can we take her home?" Emmit asked.

"We have to take more x-rays before I can say for sure. She's going to have some rough days ahead of her, and, of course. she'll need counseling. I'm sorry."

"Doctor, how bad is she really?" Emmit asked. His wide chest was heaving in and out from anger. He was a large-built man and stood with his legs apart, his arms folded against his chest.

"She has broken ribs, a broken arm, and one of her eyes is swollen so badly she can't open it. She was abused badly. There are bruises all over her body."

"Can we see her?" Betty asked, wiping tears with a tissue.

"She won't know you're here, but yes, you can see her." The doctor walked away and left the family behind him.

Lacy entered Autumn's room first and was shocked when she got to the bed. She barely recognized her sister's face. Autumn's eyes were swollen shut, and Lacy doubted if she could see even if they were open; her face was black and blue. Even while she was asleep, she looked as though she was in pain. It was painful to wonder how badly she had suffered before losing consciousness. Lacy spun around when she heard Betty cry out.

"If I ever meet up with the man who harmed my daughter, I swear I'll kill him," Emmit said. He bent over and kissed Autumn's cheek and held her small, lifeless hand in his.

Betty sat on the edge of the bed and stared at Autumn's battered face. She knew that Autumn had met the wrong man. She had often wondered where

Autumn met her men, and prayed that she would be safe. But most of all, Betty prayed that she was cured and had beaten the sinful disease. She had convinced herself that Autumn had stopped; after all, she was getting married.

Autumn had changed from the exultant woman who loved teaching to an individual whose illness was destroying her life. Now Betty was worried about Autumn's state of mind, and what her condition would be when she woke up. What happened, why did she feel the need to go out again, and how could Betty explain it to Emmit? She didn't want him to know of Autumn's illness and the sexual partners she had picked up. Betty stood up and walked out of the room. *Lord, why aren't Autumn and Matthew getting married, what has happened?* Betty had so many unanswered questions and no one to answer them except Autumn. Once she was outside, she held her head in her hands and cried for her daughter's unhappiness.

Chapter 4

"Mom, you have to tell Daddy," Lacy whispered. "You should have told him when Autumn first developed sex addiction." She was tired of the secrets and lies, and her sister's double life. It was Betty who didn't want Emmit to know, and now he had to find out in such a repulsive way and at a time of sorrowfulness.

Lacy took a seat next to Betty. "Let's face it, Mom. Daddy blamed you for Autumn being sexually abused because it was your brother who did it. He was wrong for blaming you. It wasn't your fault. Now she's not getting married, and there will be more questions asked. Dad needs to know before she's awake. When she's well enough, she may tell him anyway. It's best that you tell him first."

"Oh, God. Now she may tell him. I'll tell him today. Emmit is going to be angry enough to kill me, but I did what I thought was best. Besides, Autumn didn't want him to know either, so it wasn't all me."

As Lacy thought about it, she didn't remember Autumn telling her that she didn't want their father to know, but Lacy didn't mention that. Lacy was sure that it was Betty's idea.

Emmit rushed out the room. "She's awake. Autumn is awake," he shouted with excitement.

Betty and Lacy looked at each other then rushed to Autumn's room, but her eyes were closed again.

"Emmit, did she say anything?" Betty asked with a glimmer of hope.

"Yes. She tried to look at me and said that she was sorry. Imagine my girl apologized for being hurt. Isn't that just like Autumn?"

"Yes, that's just like Autumn, all right. Leave it to her, and she will apologize till the end," Lacy replied sarcastically. She looked away when Betty raised one brow with a defiant glare.

Betty took a closer look at Autumn's face. How could another human be so cruel? Her daughter must have been in extreme pain, and Betty wondered how she lived through it. She sat in the chair next to the bed and watched her closely.

"Autumn, are you awake?" Betty looked up at Emmit with hope in her eyes. "She tightened her grip around my hand."

"Mom?" Autumn scarcely whispered.

"I'm here, baby." Betty kissed her on the forehead. "I'm here, baby."

"Please don't be too disappointed with me. I'm so sorry," she whispered.

"What is the girl talking about, Betty?" Emmit asked as he stepped closer to the bed. Betty and Lacy exchanged glances but didn't answer.

"Sleep, baby. Don't try to talk," Betty said.

"If she can talk let her tell us what happened, Betty. The police need to know if she can describe the person who hurt her, and frankly, I want to know myself. What are you sorry for, Autumn?" Emmit urged.

Autumn closed her eyes. "She's too tired, Emmit. Let the poor girl sleep," Betty insisted.

Unable to speak, Lacy watched in silence and was glad to see the doctor return. "She spoke to my mom, and fell back to sleep again," Lacy spoke up. She had to get the family home so they could talk. Emmit needed to know what really happened to Autumn. It was time that Betty told him.

"Good. She needs to sleep off the medication before she can tell you anything," the doctor said. "I'm surprised she regained consciousness tonight. But at least she recognized her family. You should go home and get some rest then come back later. By then she may be able to tell you more. The police officers want to see her when she awakes."

Lacy stepped forward. "Mom, I'll go home with you for a while, then I need to get Jordan off to school."

On the way home, Betty and Emmit were quiet. Betty watched Emmit as he went slowly to the bedroom. Betty went to the kitchen to make coffee. Lacy walked in behind them and sat at the dining room table.

"Daddy, Mom, we need to talk." Lacy just wanted to get it over with so she could go home. After Emmit was told, Betty would be left to soften the blow. After all, it was Betty who'd kept the secret, as always.

Emmit went back to the living room before Betty. He sat on the sofa and stared straight ahead. He looked so sad; Lacy went to sit close to him and hold his hand.

"She did wake for a minute, Dad. She will again. You and Mom need some sleep. But now we need to talk. Mom, come out here please." Lacy was now standing, waiting for Betty. "Now, Mom," she yelled again.

Betty didn't answer, and Emmit looked irritated.

"Mom," Lacy shouted again.

Betty finally came to the living room and placed a cup of coffee on the table in front of Emmit. "Lacy there's more coffee in the kitchen if you want some."

"Thanks, Mom. But I can wait until I get home. Dad, there is something that you need to know."

"No, Lacy," Betty said, almost dropping her cup on the table. Coffee spilled on the front of her dress. "It can wait."

"We've waited too long already, Mom. Dad, Matthew and Autumn won't be getting married. He left her last night.

"This is going to be a shock, but I'm certain that Autumn didn't know the person who harmed her last night. You see, she has sex addiction, and has been going to bars picking up men for sex. She was going to her support group, but I guess she stopped. I'm sure she'll start back again when she gets better. It's important that she goes back as soon as possible. I think she will continue this time and not stop just because she wants to. Autumn will have to learn she can't do everything she wants. If she would have continued, she wouldn't have been hurt." There, she'd said it and she waited for Emmit's reaction. But he just stared at her. Speechless and shocked, he stared at Lacy as though he was looking straight through her. She wondered if he understood what she had said to him.

"What are you saying, Lacy? Are you telling me that Autumn's been whoring around and picking up men?" His hand trembled and coffee spilled as he placed the cup back on the table. He wiped his forehead with the napkin. Betty started to get up, but he held her back.

"No. She's no whore and don't you ever call her that again. How could you, Emmit? She's your daughter."

"I didn't say she was, and how long have you known this, Betty?" Emmit shouted, and she trembled.

Betty held her head up. "Two years. She came to me two years ago. But she had gotten better until a few months ago."

"Why didn't you tell me? I'm her father, damn you. You had no right to keep it from me. I'll never forgive you, Betty." For a stunned instant, it seemed as though he would slap her, but he quickly stood up and stormed out the door, slamming it hard behind him.

Betty ran out behind him. "Emmit, come back here," she yelled, but he didn't answer. He got inside his car and drove away. Betty went back inside the house and stood in front of Lacy. "Well, did you enjoy yourself?" she shouted, and rushed straight to her bedroom.

Lacy looked after Betty. Why was her mother angry with her? She wasn't the one who was sleeping around. And she told Betty more than once to discuss the matter with her father. But Betty did everything her way, with little regard for her husband's feeling.

Chapter 5

She had screamed for the fifth time. The nurses would come running into her room, then she would fall back into a slumber. The nightmare was always the same: she was being beaten and raped. And just when she thought the beatings were unbearable, she fainted. Thank the Good Lord that she fainted.

Lacy didn't go to her job that day, and it was four o'clock when she drove Betty back to the hospital. Emmit hadn't returned home, and they had no idea where he was.

"Lacy when you go home you need to rest. There's nothing you can do for Autumn anyway. For an amazingly short span of time so much has happened, and I don't know if Emmit will ever forgive me."

"He will in due time, Mom. Right now he's shocked and angry, and maybe feels that you've deceived him." Lacy parked the car and they went inside the hospital.

"I didn't deceive him. I wasn't sure if he could handle his daughter having sex addiction. That's not an easy thing for a father to swallow about his daughter. I did what I thought was right."

"It wasn't right, Mom. I told you that more than once."

Once they arrived on the correct floor, Betty asked the nurse if Emmit had been back, but he hadn't.

After watching Autumn for twenty minutes, Lacy decided to go down the hall and buy herself a Coke. When she returned to Autumn's room, Betty was still sitting in the same spot. She looked drained and was wiping tears from her eyes.

"Did she wake up at all?"

"No. I'm worried. The nurse said that she is having terrible nightmares. She screams in her sleep. Just now she flinched like she was in pain and cried out. How could Emmit not be here?"

"After coming damn near being beaten to death, I would say it's natural to have nightmares and be screaming out loud. At least we know she's alive and will get better," Lacy answered.

"You're right. She is alive. I wonder when Matthew found out about Autumn's illness. I'm surprised he hadn't found out before now."

"I guess she covered her tracks pretty good," Lacy said. "And being a doctor he works all hours of the night. Autumn could easily go out anytime of night and be home without Matthew knowing she had left."

"Emmit, she's going to ask why you aren't there."

"I can't look at her, Betty. All this time, Autumn has been sleeping with different men and I didn't know. Who knows how many men she's had? I love my daughter, but I can't look at her right now." Emmit was at the kitchen table drinking a cup of coffee. Betty sat opposite him with her hands folded on the table in front of her. She was losing her patience with Emmit. Didn't he understand that his daughter could have been killed? "What do I tell her when she asks about you?"

"Why don't you think of something to tell her, Betty, since you've decided what's right for everyone in this family. She may have kept going to her meetings if I would have known. But you kept the most important problem in our family a secret, and it wasn't right for you to convince Lacy to keep it from me, too. After forty years of marriage, it will never be the same between us, and I'll never trust you again." He stood up and went to the window, turning his back to her as she spoke.

"That's right, hide from it. That's why I didn't tell you. I knew that I would be the one to handle Autumn's problem when it got too rough for you. I have to solve every problem in this family."

"That's not true and you know it. I now realize that I should have put a stop to your disrespect a long time ago. But I loved you and wanted you to be happy. This time you've gone too far. When I retired from the Army, I knew that you were used to handling all the problems in the family because I was always away. I came home, and made the mistake of leaving it that way. I might have been able to protect my daughter if you had told me, Betty. Now, I can't look at either of you." He walked out of the kitchen, but Betty followed.

"If you can't forgive me, I don't blame you. But for Autumn's sake I promised to keep it a secret. I knew that it would have disappointed and hurt you, Emmit. Autumn didn't want that either."

"Well, thanks to you, I'm hurt, and disappointed,

but it's because of you." Emmit didn't say that he was hurt and disappointed in Autumn, too. He had no right to be, but he was.

Betty was tired of trying to explain it to a deaf ear. She had enough worries to last her a lifetime. "So what excuse are you going to give her for not going to the hospital?"

"I don't know. For the next two weeks I will be working late. In her condition, she'll probably be asleep when I get off work. Tell her whatever you want to."

"You are working late to avoid seeing Autumn? How can you, Emmit?"

"For all the obvious reasons. I can't get it out of my mind that she's been living like a whore." It tore his heart in two to think of Autumn sleeping around with so many men. He should have been told so he could have protected her.

Betty stared at him as though she couldn't believe what he had said. The family she had so carefully structured together was crumbling apart before her. Speechless, she turned on her heels and walked out the door.

Betty went to the patio and took a seat where it was peaceful. She thought of how different her two daughters were. Autumn cared for everyone, and she loved to teach. She made a decent salary, and could save more money than anyone Betty knew. Her clothes were mostly bought from Macy's, and soon she would move into one of the new homes being built in Inglewood. Whereas Lacy lived in a three-bedroom house in Westchester and shopped in the more expensive stores. Anyone who saw her knew that she had expensive taste. She went to the beauty salon every week, then to the nail shop. Betty often wondered if Lacy's husband objected to her excessive spending. Betty went into the yard to pick up the grapefruit off the ground. The tree was full of them.

Lacy drove six blocks before she realized that Betty hadn't spoken to her. She had been quiet, and quiet wasn't one of Betty's best attributes. She talked more than anyone that Lacy knew.

"Will Dad be home earlier tonight?"

"No. He made an excuse that he has to work late for a few weeks. I'm so damn disgusted with the way he is handling the situation with Autumn. He acts as though she could control it. I gave up on him." Betty looked out the window to hide her tears.

"You know, Mom, I think it's hard for fathers to deal with the fact that their daughters are sleeping with different men. They can't accept us dating or going out like they would with a son. He probably feels that in some way he could have protected her. I wish that I would have told him, but you told me not to. I should have known better."

Betty turned around in her seat. "Oh, so you agree that it's all my fault?"

"No. But I shouldn't have agreed to keep it a secret from Dad. I should have told him. She is his daughter, too." Lacy knew she shouldn't have listened to Betty or Autumn. Now, everything was a mess. The ride to the hospital had become tense and resentful, and Lacy knew it was because she had told Emmit the truth about Autumn's double life.

"When Autumn finally told me that Reggie had been sexually abusing her, I was sure that I would die. My own damn brother; how could he do such a thing? Too bad Autumn didn't tell us until he died. I would have killed him if he were still alive. I didn't even get a chance to slap his face. When I took her for counseling she refused to talk about it, or what she was feeling. I kept telling myself that if she would have talked about it and not kept it inside for so long, maybe that terrible illness wouldn't have developed inside her." Betty pulled tissues from her purse to wipe her eyes. She could see the hospital from a short distance.

"I know, Mom. But you have to let Dad in, and stop handling everything the way you want to. And Autumn shouldn't have stopped attending her meetings. This is what happens when she thinks she can do whatever the hell she wants to."

Betty looked at Lacy. She sounded cold, and unsympathetic.

Autumn was in bed waiting when Lacy and Betty arrived. The nurse had helped her dress to go home.

"How do you feel, honey?" Betty asked.

"Like I'm living in my last days. When I breathe my ribs hurt, I can't use my right arm, and my body looks as though I was kicked for ten miles. It's hard to look at myself in the mirror. I wish that I could go to my apartment and lock the doors."

"In a couple of weeks you will feel better," Lacy said. She looked at the tray of food beside the bed. "Can I have the apple? I had to miss lunch to come here."

"Sure. Take anything you want." Autumn was disappointed that Emmit wasn't there. But she realized he did work long hours, and in the evenings he was tired.

Still, she needed him, and she needed his forgiveness and understanding. "I'll need a wheelchair."

"The nurse said she would get it. I just want you home so I can take care of you," Betty said. She looked at her daughter; the puffy face that was black and blue and the swollen eyes made her heart ache. But she had to be strong for Autumn. Crying would only make Autumn feel worse.

The nurse entered the room with the wheelchair. "All set to go?"

"Yes," Autumn answered. Knowing her ribs would pain her enormously, she braced herself and tried to hold her breath as the nurse and Betty each grabbed an arm. "Wait, wait. It's too painful." But before Autumn could decline any further, she was placed in the chair. "Oh, God, it hurts," she cried.

Lacy just stared, sorry for all the pain Autumn felt. "Does it hurt that much?"

"Yes, Lacy. I have some broken ribs," Autumn snapped.

Lacy and Betty would have to help her out of the car and into the house, which would be painful.

They helped Autumn into the car, and she screamed again as she was placed in the front seat. Getting into the wheelchair and the car had been painful, but the car ride home was even worse. She felt every bump and turn; she didn't think that she would ever be pain free again. Lord, how she wished her father were here to help her. But the pain was her punishment, and her reminder to value and reclaim her priorities again. Her life had been changed.

The ride home was quiet, aside from the sounds of Autumn's pain, but helping Autumn into the house and into bed was worse than climbing outside the car. Emmit was at work, so Lacy and Betty had to help her.

"I'll get a glass of water and your pain pills," Betty said, and went into the kitchen. She left Autumn and Lacy in the bedroom that they shared as children.

Lacy walked around the room. "It still looks the same."

"What's the matter, Lacy? You know that I sense it when you are angry or trying to keep something inside. You can't sit in one place when it happens."

Lacy was facing Autumn as she perched on the other twin bed. "Mom didn't tell Dad about your sex addiction."

"I know, and she told me not to."

"That's what I figured. Why you listen to everything she says, I will never know. She lied and said that you didn't want him to know. Well, he had to know and he knows now. I told him. That should teach her a lesson. She wants to be in control of everything, and everyone."

"It's okay. I was going to tell him tonight anyway. It will save me the embarrassment. What did he say?"

"He's angry. Very angry with Mom; they're not speaking. Right now he's angry with all of us, and I had nothing to do with it. Though I can't blame him. He has the right to be angry."

"Is he ignoring you, too?"

"No, but I'm sure he will ignore you. Can you imagine how he felt when I told him that you were probably beaten by a man that you picked up for sex? I should have told him before."

"Yes, I can imagine, Lacy." Autumn held her head down.

"Anyway, he's been working long hours so I haven't

seen him." Lacy knew that Emmit was avoiding her as well, but she couldn't say it to Autumn. She would find out soon enough. "Here, let me fluff your pillows so you can be comfortable." After Lacy fluffed the pillows she took a set of keys from her purse. "Your car is parked inside your garage."

"You've been busy helping me, Lacy. But it will be the last time I will ever put my family through this again. I'm so ashamed of my actions." Autumn tried to relax, but the pain in her ribs was unbearable.

"So that means you will go back to attending your meetings?"

"As soon as I can get out of bed and drive without doubling over."

"I spoke with Matthew the night you were hurt."

Autumn held her head down and closed her eyes. The night Matthew left her was like yesterday. "He hates me, Lacy. Of all the people, you called him," she said angrily.

"Why wouldn't I call him? You were hurt, and you and Matthew were going to be married. It's only natural that I would call him." Lacy sounded as though her feelings were hurt.

Autumn placed both hands over her face and pushed her hair back. "I know you were right to call him, but he could care less what happens to me. I can't say that I blame him. No one knows the hell I've lived for the past year. Hiding, and hating who I had become, and degrading myself. This disease that's inside me almost cost me my life. It rules me. No matter how hard I try, I have no control over it." She stopped to wipe her eyes and control the sobs before Betty came to her room. She felt sweat on her forehead and wiped it off with the back of her hand.

"I've had terrible nightmares of the beating. In every nightmare I died and woke up crying."

"You'll have to forget Matthew."

"It's easier said than done. I was so wrong for not telling him."

"Even if you told him, he still wouldn't marry you. Matthew is too caught up in his career and what other people think."

"But he would have had a choice, and at least he could say that I was honest. Now, he doesn't have an ounce of respect for me. Believe me, he does hate me."

"It's over between you and Matthew. Now you have to concentrate on getting well and putting your life back together. I'm sorry to say it, but Matthew will never come back to you, so don't expect him to," Lacy said bluntly. "Autumn, was it more than one who hurt you?"

Autumn folded her arms and lowered her eyes. "It was two, but that's not what I wanted. I knew nothing about the second one. Two brothers set me up, and I was scared to death."

Lacy watched the tears spill from Autumn's eyes, and she shivered. "We don't have to talk about it now."

"Thanks. But I'm not sure that I will ever be able to talk about it without crying and reliving that night. And I'm in so much pain that I can barely breathe. I need another pain pill."

"I'm coming with your pain pill," Betty said as she entered the bedroom with a glass of water in her hand.

"Lacy, go home and get some rest. You look tired and you need to be home with your family."

"Okay, Mom. Call me if you need me to do anything."

Betty walked Lacy to the door. "Everything will work out when Autumn is feeling better."

"I hope so, Mom." Lacy kissed Betty on the cheek and walked out. Once Lacy was outside, she looked at the roses in Betty's yard. The spring was coming, and soon the roses would explode with color and scent. She felt a tear on her face and was happy for the husband she had. Eric and Jordan were everything she wanted in her life. She and Eric had been married for ten years, and the passion and love was still there. She hoped that one day Autumn would be as happy as she was.

Autumn took the pain pill and asked Betty to close the door on her way out of the room. She wanted to be alone and didn't want Betty or anyone asking questions. Besides, the medication would make her sleep. But until it took effect, the pain in her ribs was more than enough to bear.

She woke up with a start and screamed. She couldn't remember where she was. Was she in a motel? Had she been left alone and fallen asleep? Immediately after the sex, she always dressed without idle conversation and went straight home to shower. Sometimes she would soak in the bathtub for an hour. She had to wash away the memory. As she rose up too quickly from the bed, the pain went all through her body and she gradually remembered that she was in her parents' home.

The blinds were open and the darkness had approached. She remembered the brutal beating and the mens' faces and she screamed again, pulling the blanket over her face.

After an hour, Autumn heard Betty's angry voice. It sounded as though she was arguing with Emmit.

"What do you want me to tell Autumn? Her feelings will be hurt, and Emmit, you can't avoid her forever. Her illness is a disease and not a hobby, and she can't help it. Don't you think she tried?"

Autumn's heart dropped. Her father had the same opinion of her as Matthew did. She felt as though her life had fallen apart. She could live with Matthew's opinion of her, but not her father's. "Not Daddy," she whispered. How could she face him again?

Chapter 6

When Lacy woke up Eric had already left. She went into the kitchen to fix Jordan's lunch when she heard the doorbell rang. Lacy frowned and wondered who was at the door at seven in the morning. She dried her hands with the dish towel and rushed out of the kitchen.

"Yes?" she opened the door.

The visitor looked at Lacy for seconds before answering. "My name is Tammy. Are you Lacy Patterson?"

"Yes, I am. How can I help you?" Lacy glanced behind her to see if Jordan was eating his breakfast. They had to leave by eight. Then she studied the seriousness of the young woman's face. She was cute, about twenty-one, maybe twenty-two, and she was shivering in the cold weather. Lacy watched her as she pushed her hands into her coat pockets.

"I'm pregnant, and the baby is Eric's." She held her breath waiting for Lacy's response. Had she made a mistake by coming here? Her mother had told her not to, but her friends said to tell his wife. She needed to know what a jerk she was married to.

For a moment it seemed as though the earth stood still, and Lacy felt a sensation of numbness before panic crept rapidly down her spine. No one spoke, no one moved. They looked into each other's eyes waiting for the other's reaction.

Finally, and with effort, Lacy cleared her throat. "How old are you?"

"Twenty years old, and six months' pregnant. Eric knows, but he hasn't returned my calls. Like it or not, he will support his baby."

Lacy shifted on one leg. "Let me get this straight. You are carrying my husband's baby? He won't return any of your calls, so why in hell are you here? Is it to hurt me? Why?" For Jordan's sake, she tried to keep her voice even, but she felt as though she would lose control. She looked at the face of the young woman, sixteen years younger than she was.

"No, Lacy. I'm not trying to hurt you."

"It's Mrs. Patterson," Lacy snapped.

"No. I'm not trying to hurt you, Mrs. Patterson. But after I told Eric that I was pregnant, he didn't want to see me anymore. If I was good enough for him to sleep with, then he will support this baby. You tell him that." She shivered again and pulled her coat tightly around her protruding stomach.

For a stunned instant Lacy wanted to slap Tammy hard across her face. She had broken up her marriage, and Lacy had had no suspicion that Eric had cheated on her. Looking in Tammy's face made more anger build inside of Lacy. She hated this young woman, and at that moment she hated Eric as well. Unable to speak or move, Lacy just stared at Tammy.

Tammy stood for a few seconds and watched Lacy as she saw the tears forming in her eyes, the raw hatred on her face, and the trembling of her hands, then Tammy turned swiftly and hurried back to her car. There was no more that she could do here. But one thing was for sure, Eric would call her tonight. She was sure of that.

Lacy watched Tammy as she drove away in her white Honda. She closed the door and was glad to see that Jordan hadn't come out of the kitchen and she didn't have to face him right then. She flopped down on the sofa and watched both hands tremble as she folded her arms against her chest to try and stop the shivering. She needed someone to hold her before she fell apart; Lacy closed her eyes, wondering what to do about the situation. Thirty-six years old tomorrow, and she was already tired, so very tired.

Lacy called her office and said that she wasn't feeling well and wouldn't be in that day. She paced the living room, held both hands over her face, and shook her head in disbelief. A baby, she thought. Eric had been quiet lately, but she hadn't for a moment imagined him getting someone pregnant. She knew what she had to do. First, she would take Jordan to school. Then she would go to Eric's job and confront him. If he admitted that he'd cheated on her, she would come home, pack his clothes, and change the locks on the doors. She threw both hands in the air. What was she thinking? Of course he had cheated on her, and worse, a baby was on the way. She could accept the cheating, but not the baby. No, there wasn't anything that Eric could do to change it and make her forgive him. How many times had he cheated on her; was Tammy the first?

Lacy stopped in front of her son's school, kissed him on his cheek, and drove off to the Aerospace Company in El Segundo, California. She would confront Eric and make it quick. Her nerves were eating at her stomach. She was too shocked to cry, but was livid with rage that was killing her inside. She needed to scream, cry, or—most of all—she needed to strike out at Eric.

Lacy parked her car and started toward Eric's office. Someone spoke to her, but she walked fast, without looking in the faces of anyone around her.

When she entered Eric's office, he looked up from the printout that lay open on the desk in front of him and frowned as she slammed the door closed.

Eric stood up behind his desk. "Lacy, what's wrong? Oh no, it's not Jordan?"

"No, Eric, it's not Jordan. I have two words to say to you, "Tammy's baby."

Eric's jaws tightened; he pushed the report aside, rushed around his desk, and stopped in front of Lacy. He grabbed both her hands. "Lacy, it's not what you think. It lasted only one month and I stopped seeing her because I loved you, baby."

She pulled her hands from his hold. "So it is your baby, and you've made me look like a fool. You cheated, lied, and betrayed my trust. And you know what, I loved you more than the day we were married." Unable to endure facing him any longer, she turned her back to him.

"It doesn't have to be my baby. I mean, it may

belong to someone else. You can't let one mistake come between us." He squinted his eyes as he watched her face fill with accusation.

"You did, Eric. You let one mistake come between us when you cheated," she answered.

He was standing close to her and didn't see it coming until she slapped him hard across his face. She turned around to walk out the door, but he grabbed her arm.

"I know you're angry now, but it's you I love. Tonight we will talk about this. Just tell me what you want me to do, Lacy. I'll do anything, please."

She saw tears in his eyes, but she didn't care, and she pulled away from him again. "There isn't anything that you can do now but go back to that little bitch. You made your bed, so sleep in it." She started to the door.

Eric rushed to her side. He couldn't let her go without her forgiveness. "Honey, you can't mean that. I want to go home with you, but I have a report that's due today. I can't leave early. But when I get home, we have to find a way to work this problem out. I can't lose my family over a terrible mistake that I made only once."

Lacy realized that she was leaving without her purse and grabbed it off his desk, then opened the door widely. "If you loved me so much, you wouldn't have gotten another woman pregnant." There was no use staying any longer, and the damage was done— to her, to their family and marriage. She had been true to him, was always there when he needed her, but she wouldn't be any longer. Staying with him was clearly out of the question.

Lacy drove up her driveway in Westchester,

California. She laid her head back on the seat and closed her eyes. There were so many good years in her marriage: the day of their wedding, the day she delivered Jordan. When she was in labor, Eric had said that it was an honor to have her as his wife and she believed him.

How would Eric explain to Jordan that he had a baby by another woman? Why hadn't she seen the signs, where had she been? she wondered with anger and frustration.

When they were in college, they had planned to marry. But Eric decided that they shouldn't rush. Two years after they finished school, Lacy told him they were going to either get married or date other people. After thinking it over for a day, he realized that he couldn't see her with another man and asked her to marry him. The marriage was solid, and they were happy. What had happened to make him need another woman?

Lacy blew her nose, wiped her eyes, and backed out of the driveway. She drove around the corner to Sepulveda and Manchester Boulevard to Ralph's Market and walked out with six brown boxes. Next door was a locksmith; she made arrangements to have the owner change the locks on the front and back doors before Eric came home from his office.

Once she was home, all the anger and hurt exploded into uncontrollable sobs. "How could you do this to me?" she yelled, and flopped down in the brown leather chair in the living room. "How could you ruin our lives over a complete stranger?" The ringing of the phone stopped her, but she didn't answer it. She switched on the answering machine.

"Lacy, I called your office and you weren't there.

Please pick up the phone. I know you're there. Lacy, please pick up the phone. Call me, baby."

Lacy didn't pick up the phone and she didn't return any of Eric's calls. Instead, she dragged the boxes to their bedroom and started stuffing his clothes into the boxes as though they were rags. An hour later, the locksmith arrived and changed all the locks.

After pushing all six boxes to the patio, Lacy was tired. She glanced at her watch; it was four-thirty. She was always at the after-school day-care center to pick up Jordan by five. Today she would drop him off at her parents' house until Eric came and got his clothes, and by seven she would bring Jordan home. Explaining to a seven-year-old would be hard, but she didn't have to do that tonight. Not when she was so extremely devastated.

Waiting for Eric, she paced in the living room, stopped and peeked out the window, but he wasn't there. She stopped in front of their wedding picture on the table, grabbed it, and threw it on the shiny hardwood floor; pieces of broken glass fell under the coffee table. "Go to hell, Eric." She flopped down on the sofa, and glanced at her watch again. Finally, she heard his car come up the driveway and heard him rushing to the door. The lock was changed on the black-bar door, but she opened the wood door so she could look into his eyes. She wanted to see the same hurt there that he had inflicted on her. Lacy stood at the door and waited.

"You are waiting for me, baby?" He sound relieved when he saw her.

"Yes. Your clothes are on the patio. I want you to take them and drive as far from me as possible. Go to her and never come back." She started to walk away when he placed the key inside the lock.

Eric tried to turn the key from left to right, but it didn't move. "Oh, damn. What did you do, Lacy?"

She crossed her arms in front of her. "Under the circumstances, I did the only sensible thing. I had the locks changed. You don't live here anymore, so get your clothes and leave."

"No," he yelled. "You can't do this to me. You can't destroy our family over one mistake. One damn mistake is all I've made. This is my house too, Lacy."

She stood closer to the door. "Did you say one mistake? And one baby; don't forget the baby, Eric. So don't tell me that I can't break up this family. You should have thought of that when you were pumping Tammy," she screamed and hit the bar door with her open hand. "You betrayed my trust, and you lied and used me. So don't you dare tell me what I can't do. I hate you." She slammed the door and stood against it.

"I didn't use you, Lacy. Please believe me when I say that I love you."

Lacy held her hands to her face. She heard Eric walk around the back of the house. Then she held her breath while listening to the sound of boxes being thrown in his black Ford SUV.

Lacy went to the phone and dialed Betty's number. "Mom, please tell Jordan to be ready. I'm leaving to pick him up. Oh, and Mom, tell him I'm not coming inside so be ready to come out to the car." Lacy's eyes were puffy and red, and she wasn't in any mood to explain why. Betty would only ask hundreds of questions that she wasn't prepared to answer.

Chapter 7

Two weeks had passed since Autumn was released from the hospital. Under the circumstances, Autumn was recovering well and walking on her own. Betty had returned to the beauty salon, but was accepting only her regular clients so she could spend more time with Autumn.

It was eight-fifteen and Betty had fallen asleep. Autumn combed her hair and slipped into her bathrobe. She went into the living room to wait for Emmit. Tonight she was determined to talk to him. Once and for all he would have to say more than just a casual hello and make excuses for the long day's work, then go straight to his room. On the weekends, he worked Saturdays and spent most of Sunday at church and saying as little as possible to her. She was tired of his avoiding her, and she would not stay in his home any longer unless he could come clean and tell her what was on his mind. She knew he was disappointed, but they had to discuss it. She had to make him understand. Emmit had always been a reasonable, quiet, levelheaded man.

Autumn heard him place the key in the door. She was standing close by when he walked in.

Emmit was a tall man, 6'3", and well over two hundred pounds. Since retiring from the Army he'd worked as an engineer at TRW Aerospace in Manhattan Beach. He opened the door quietly and stopped when he faced Autumn and saw the disconsolate look on her face.

"Shouldn't you be in bed, Autumn? It hasn't been that long since you were hurt."

"I probably should, Dad. But not until we talk about what's troubling you. You haven't said more than ten words to me since I've been here. I'm starting to think that I'm not welcome and should go home to recover."

"Autumn, I'm tired. I've worked twelve hours every day for the last two weeks." He stepped past her.

"You would work twelve hours to avoid your daughter?"

Emmit stopped but didn't turn around to face her. He hadn't been able to look her in the eyes since he found out about the life she had been living. Maybe someone else's daughter, but his daughters didn't sleep around with a different man every night. His daughters went to church and taught school, and Lacy had a son and a good marriage.

"I'm sorry that I couldn't help you, Autumn. You, Betty, or Lacy never told me what was going on with you, and no one gave me a chance to protect you when you needed me. You have no idea how it makes a father feel."

She stepped in front of him. "Dad, I'm an adult now, and there wasn't anything that you could have done to keep me safe. I was too ashamed to tell you. But I sure didn't think that you would isolate me from your life once you found out."

Emmit saw her wipe the tears off her cheek and wanted to hold her in his arms, but he couldn't reach out to her. "Right now I feel very insignificant, and not needed by my family." Autumn sat on the sofa and Emmit sat next to her. "My wife doesn't respect or trust me enough to confide in me about my own daughters. I thought we had a marriage, but I was mistaken. Maybe I was away too much when you girls were growing up."

"You've been a terrific father and husband. But it's hard for any woman to tell her father she has sex addiction. I made Mom and Lacy promise to keep my secret. That was the only reason you didn't know." Autumn lied, but she had to make him feel better. It was Betty who'd insisted Autumn keep the sex addiction a secret. "But you can be here for me now, Dad. I need your support, and I want my old life back." She pulled a tissue from her pocket and wiped the tear off Emmit's face. It broke her heart to see what she had done to him.

Emmit was facing her. He hadn't even realized the tears were there until she wiped his face, and he took her hand and pulled her into his arms.

His arms felt strong, and Autumn felt safe again. She closed her eyes and lay her head on his shoulder.

From their bedroom, Betty watched her husband and daughter. She listened as the two talked and cried. But she and Emmit still had issues to work out in their marriage. She had to be the strong one in the family for him and their daughters. Betty wondered if he had forgiven her as well. But from what she heard him say to Autumn, she didn't think he would let her off the hook as easily.

Betty saw Emmit leaving the living room, and she ran back to bed to pretend that she was still sleeping. She listened as he came toward their bedroom, but he passed the door and went into the den where he had been sleeping for two weeks.

"Hi, Mom. Is Autumn asleep?" Lacy asked as she entered the living room.

"No. She stays up all day since she can get around on her own. It's hard to keep her in bed. She's recovering well, Lacy. Where is Jordan?" Betty looked over Lacy's shoulder.

"He's with Eric." They heard Autumn's footsteps and turned around to see her entering. She walked slowly and lightly on her feet.

"You seem to be doing much better, Autumn. How is the pain in your ribs?" Lacy asked.

"It's still there, but I had to get out of bed sooner or later. Next week I think that I can go home."

"Oh no, Autumn. It's still too soon." Betty protested.

"No, it's not too soon, Mom. I want to be in my own apartment, and if I'm careful I can take care of myself."

Betty and Lacy looked at each other. Autumn had been snappy for the past three days. Betty was afraid that maybe she was getting the urge for sex and needed to go to her meetings soon.

"I'm sorry, Mom. I'm just tired of being in constant pain, and I miss going to work. I've been cooped up inside for weeks now."

Lacy sighed. "Well, I have some bad news myself. Eric isn't living at home. I threw him out a week ago."

"What?" Betty asked. "A week and you hadn't said anything about it."

"Yes, Mom, a week. I couldn't talk about it before."

"I'm so sorry, Lacy. What is going on with the women in this family?" Autumn asked. "What happened, if you don't mind me asking?"

"Of course she doesn't mind. We are concerned about you, and what about Jordan. How is he taking it?" Betty asked. "Jordan and Eric are very close. One thing that I can say for Eric, he is a good father. If he doesn't come home soon, Jordan will become devastated if he's not already."

"He doesn't understand, of course. But I assured him that there hadn't been any talk of divorce, though I will be filing for one. A young woman came to my house and told me that she was carrying Eric's child. When I asked him, he admitted that they had been together. I will never forgive him for breaking up our family, and I can never trust him again."

Betty gaped, sighed, and shook her head in disbelief. "I'm surprised that Eric could be so stupid. I feel like knocking him on his head with my fist. Maybe it's not even his baby. You never know. She has a lot of nerve coming to your home. She did it for you to throw Eric out, and she'll be waiting for him." Betty didn't understand what was happening to her daughter's life. In an amazingly short span of time, everything had changed.

"It doesn't matter. He cheated on me, Mom. I don't want him anymore."

"'You sound so final and angry, Lacy."

"You're damn right I'm angry, Autumn. Wouldn't you be?"

"Yes, I would." She looked at Lacy and noticed that she looked tired. Lacy's skin was dark brown, and she had black hair, slanted dark eyes, and a full mouth; she was a very attractive woman. As Autumn listened to the changes in Lacy's life, she wondered what her own future would be.

"I have to learn to live without a husband in the house with me. I thought that we would be married forever, but nothing seems to be certain in my life right now. Your face isn't swollen anymore, Autumn. Soon the bruises will be gone."

Autumn sensed that it was too painful for Lacy to discuss her marriage any longer. "I'll be happy when I can go to the beauty salon, and I need to make an appointment with my dermatologist. I don't think all the bruises on my face are going to heal without leaving scars." Inadvertently, she raised her hand to her face and traced a line along her jaw then blinked back tears. Lacy and Betty watched her quietly.

"I believe the scars will go away," Lacy said.

"Maybe on the outside with a doctor's help, but never on the inside. They will be there forever," she answered absentmindedly. She looked straight ahead as though her mind had trailed off to a long journey.

Lacy stood up. "Well, I just thought that I would drop by to see if you needed anything and to let you know what was going on in my life."

"Does Eric want to come home?" Betty finally asked.

"Yes. He wants to waltz right back into my life and we're just supposed to pick up where we left off.

I can't do that; with my luck it will turn out to be his baby."

"And if it's not his baby, what will you do then?' Autumn asked. "You two have a son at home who loves his mom and dad very much. Maybe you should hold off on the divorce until he has proof the child is his."

"I know. I have a lot to think about. But right now, I don't see a future for Eric and me."

Mentally depressed, Betty sat in silence and watched her daughters. Both were unhappy and suffering with loss and pain. She was so sure that Lacy and Eric would be together forever, and Autumn would soon be getting married, but their lives were falling apart. There had to be something that she could do to help.

Autumn stood up. "I need to rest. I'll be in my room. Remember what I said, Lacy. Don't be in a hurry to get a divorce. I wish that I could be more help, but my own life is screwed up big time. Most of the time I hate opening my eyes in the mornings. And when they're closed I see Matthew in front of me." That was the truth of the matter. She did hate waking up to her present life.

"Emmit, Lacy came over today. She and Eric are separated." Betty went to the den and Emmit followed.

"What did you say?"

"You heard me correctly. Lacy threw Eric out of the house. Now don't say that I kept it a secret from you." She flipped on the TV.

"Did Lacy tell you not to tell me?" Emmit sat on the sofa next to Betty.

"No, she didn't, but she's pretty upset."

"Lord, what happened? What in Pete's sake brought this on?"

"The stupid fool got some woman pregnant." Betty rested her elbows on her knees and ran her fingers through her hair. She had just gotten it French-braided and it was too tight at her temples. "Our daughters are grown women. I thought we could have some peace once they were adults. I'm tired, Emmit. It's too much drama for me."

"How did Lacy find out? Did he tell her?"

"The woman had the audacity to go to their house. Eric had gone to work, but Lacy was still there. All this happened a week ago. I don't know how Eric could be so stupid," Betty said and rubbed her tired eyes. She knew that she wouldn't get much sleep. "She's already talking about filing for a divorce. But I told her to wait. No need to do something out of anger."

Emmit took his hat off and placed it on his knee, then scratched the top of his head.

Betty looked at the clock. "It's only six-thirty and you're home?" she asked, surprised.

"I was too tired to stay any later. How is Autumn?"

"She wants to go home next week. I think it's too soon, but I guess she wants to be alone. She's depressed, Emmit. She comes out of that room to get a glass of water, or make a sandwich, then she goes back to the bedroom and closes the door. She doesn't eat well, and she is getting more withdrawn every day. Her conversations on the phone are short and blunt." That day Betty had looked at Autumn closely. Her caramel-colored face was drawn and she kept her hair brushed back from her face. Even when she wore her bathrobe you could see that she had lost a tremendous amount of weight, and the bruises were still on her face and neck. Her dark, slanted eyes were vacant, empty, and sad.

"You and I need to go to church, Emmit, so we can pray for our girls. You've missed the last two Sundays."

"You know that I've been working late, and some Saturdays. I was too tired, and Sunday was the only day that I could rest."

"I know. But we do need to go and pray. I'm going to bed now. Are you coming?"

"No. I want to watch TV."

Betty didn't answer, and she knew that Emmit wasn't coming to bed with her, but she asked anyway. She was surprised that he was even talking to her, but it was only because it was about their daughters. Lately, their conversations were modest. Emmit had very little to say to her.

It was Sunday. Dreading that she had a phone call, Autumn let it ring four times before she picked up. She didn't want to talk to anyone but Matthew. It was Lacy.

"You didn't go to church?" Autumn asked.

"No. Jordan has a cold. I was thinking of you going home tomorrow. Why don't you come and stay with me for a week. I could certainly use the company. How about it, Autumn? You'll be alone during the day, and we can be together at night."

"I don't know. I'm sure I need to be home to return calls, and go through my mail."

"We can stop at your apartment and pick up your

mail, and you can check your messages. Besides, I want to attend the meetings with you when you are able to go."

Autumn took a few seconds to think it over. Maybe if she had someone to talk to she may feel better. But no one understood how she felt except someone from her group meetings. No one knew what it felt like to need sex more than food or water. But she knew that Lacy needed her, and she had been there for Autumn during this harsh period of her life.

"Okay. But only for a week, then I go home and attend my meetings."

"Good. Tell you what. I'll pick you up this afternoon, and we will go straight to your apartment, then to my house. Maybe if Mom and Dad are alone, they can patch things up between them."

"I hope so. At least they went to church together. I hate knowing they're unhappy because of me. I have to leave this house."

By noon Lacy was parking her car in the driveway and saw Autumn peeking through the drapes. Autumn opened the front door and Jordan ran into her open arms and kissed her on the cheek. She was dressed in a purple, loose-fitting dress and flat shoes.

"You are going to be taller than me soon," Autumn told Jordan.

"Where are Mom and Dad?" Lacy asked from behind Jordan.

"Mom called a half hour ago and said they were going to brunch."

"I guess that means they've made up."

"I hope so, Lacy."

"It's not because of you. It's because Mom wants to always wear the pants, and take everything in her own hands, or everything has to go her way. He's getting tired of it."

Autumn stood at the window, and Lacy took a seat in the chair. "What do you think is going to happen in their marriage?" Autumn asked with interest.

"Nothing. They've been married for forty years. Nothing will change. But I do wish Mom would stop trying to run everyone's lives and worry about her own. She left a long message on my answering machine with advice on how I should handle my marriage, then she asked if she should call Eric."

"You're kidding." Autumn wasn't surprised and was sure Betty had called Matthew.

"No, I'm not kidding. I told her not to dare call Eric. Now, so much for that. It makes me angry to think of it. Can I carry anything to the car for you? Girl, I'm happy to have you stay with us. I hate being in that big house without Eric, though I should get used to it. I'm the best thing he ever had. I still can't believe he got another woman pregnant. When we first met, he didn't have anything. I taught him class and dignity, and this is the thanks I get."

Autumn locked the door behind them and dropped the key in the mailbox. She heard it hit the floor as she closed the screen door. She had so much to deal with and wondered if she could deal with Lacy for an entire week. "Well, Mom and Dad will be alone tonight. I hope they make up."

"I hope so, too, honey. But Dad is as stubborn as a mule," Lacy said.

The first stop was Autumn's apartment. She stuck her mail inside her purse; she would read it later. Besides, it was only bills. She was disappointed that

Matthew hadn't at least sent her a get-well card. Did he even wonder if she was recovering well? While Lacy and Jordan waited in the living room, Autumn packed her overnight bags and selected two dresses from her closet that wouldn't fit tightly around her ribs or waist. As she started out of the bedroom, she stopped at the door, went back to her dresser, and opened the drawer. Autumn picked up a handful of condoms and stared at them. Then she dropped all but two in the wastepaper basket beside the dresser. She started to the door again, stopping once more, went back to the drawer and pulled out the remaining two condoms, and tossed them in the wastepaper basket. Maybe it was because of the beating, but she wanted only to reclaim the decent life she once had. She knew that she would want the sex, but with counseling, her meetings, and her family by her side, she would regain a normal sexual appetite.

"I'm all ready to go."

"Aunt Autumn, are you going to live with us forever?" Jordan asked.

"No. Just for a week." She kissed Jordan on the cheek and held his hand on their way out the door.

"I know you'll be happy when you move into a house. This apartment is so small."

"It's two bedrooms. How many rooms do you think I need, Lacy?"

"Three. You always should have three." Lacy looked at Autumn. Must be the illness that had her so snappy, she thought.

After dinner, Lacy and Autumn were in the den watching the TV and drinking coffee. Jordan was across the street at the neighbor's house with his friend.

"I'm glad I accepted your invitation. It's quiet and peaceful around here."

"Are you still looking to buy one of the new homes in Inglewood?" Lacy asked.

"Yes. I'm on the list. I like the way they're built, and I love the idea that they're in a gated community. Living alone, I'll feel safer."

Lacy sipped her coffee. "Autumn, do you really think the meetings will cure you?"

Autumn took a deep breath and sighed. "It's like being in need like an alcoholic. But it can be controlled if you really want it to. Now I have more reason to be stronger than before. I've lost the man of my dreams and was almost beaten to death. But it's more difficult than it sounds. I'm going to the meetings, and I'll have some counseling, too. This time I know that I can make it, Lacy. I can't let Dad down either." She sniffed and turned her head away.

"All my life I wanted to be a teacher and have a terrific husband and child. I still want it. It scares the hell out of me, because to the next man I fall in love with I will tell the truth about my past. And the truth is, what man wants damaged goods? No man will ever trust me. And if by some luck I meet one, he'll have to understand."

"That will be hard."

"My own father didn't understand and couldn't look me in my face when he was told. I even feel differently with him, and I'm not sure if our relationship will ever be the same again." Autumn started to cry and got up off the sofa too quickly. Her hands went to her ribs, and she bent over and moaned in pain.

"Take it easy, Autumn."

She sat back slowly. She held her breath and then tried to breathe easily until the pain subsided. "Here I'm feeling sorry for myself and discussing my problems as though you don't have any of your own. What are you going to do about Eric?"

The expression on Lacy's face went grim "I haven't decided yet. Baby or not, I'm sure that I will divorce him. How can I ever trust him again?" The phone rang, and Lacy placed her cup on the coffee table and sighed deeply. "I'll take it in my room. I know it's only Eric."

Autumn got up and glanced out the window. It was a warm, sunny day in June. She saw Jordan across the street playing with the neighbor's seven-year-old son. Autumn walked around the living room and sat at the piano, touching the keys. Lacy played the piano well, but Autumn had had no interest in learning.

"Yeah, that was him all right. He wants to see Jordan and talk with me."

"See what he has to say."

"I don't know what he could say to make me feel better or trust him with a baby on the way. A baby," she hissed. "I'm so damn embarrassed."

An hour had passed when the doorbell rang. Autumn got up to go to the spare bedroom that she would occupy. She didn't want to answer any questions. "Lacy, if Eric asks, please tell him that I'm asleep."

"Okay."

It was Eric at the door, and he was determined to reconcile his marriage. Lacy led him to the den. She didn't want to sit next to him and took a seat on the chair; Eric sat on the sofa.

"I don't know where to start," Eric said. "I've been

the biggest fool, and it hurt us, including Jordan. I didn't mean for any of it to happen, Lacy."

"Why did you feel the need to sleep with another woman?"

"That's what I've asked myself a thousand times. It wasn't a need, it was just something different for that moment."

"I hope it was worth it," Lacy snapped and turned her head away from him.

"I've always loved you, Lacy. Never doubt it. It only happened twice, but I never stopped loving you. Just think about that before you file for a divorce. While Autumn is here, do you think we can go away for the weekend? Just the two of us," he pleaded. "We can leave Jordan here with Autumn."

As Lacy looked at Eric's handsome face, she noticed the gray mingling in his sideburns. He had just left his office and was still dressed in his gray suit; his jacket lay over the arm of the sofa.

"Let me give it some thought, Eric. I'm just not sure that I could deal with you having another child." But looking at him, she knew that she was still in love with her husband and thought of him every day, and into the middle of the night. How many times had they made love and shared so much? She wondered if she should try and accept his child. After all, she had to think of Jordan's happiness and what he needed. If she did ask Eric to move back in, she knew she would forgive him. Maybe she should go away and see if the weekend would bring back the good years they had had together as a family. She decided to give him the weekend, if only for Jordan's sake.

"Okay, Eric." The phone interrupted her and she answered it.

"I know he's there because I saw his car, so don't tell me he's not. It's his baby, and I'm younger than you are and prettier. You won't have him for very long. So tell him to come to the phone."

Lacy pushed the phone into Eric's hand. "Tell her if she calls this house again, she'll be sorry. Your jacket is in the den on the sofa. Take it and anything else that belongs to you on your way out." Lacy turned to walk away. "Oh, and Eric, forget the weekend trip, or anything else you had in mind for us." She went to their bedroom and slammed the door. She was hurting even more than she did the day Tammy came to tell her about the baby. How stupid of me to consider a weekend trip with him, she thought as she leaned against the closed door and cried silently.

After Eric left, Lacy went back to the living room where Autumn was waiting for her.

"Jordan is in his room. After Eric left he cried. He wants his father home, Lacy. You should talk to him."

"I know, but it's hard on me, too. While we were talking Tammy called. I was so disgusted that I went to my bedroom. I didn't want to look at his face any longer."

"But what if the baby isn't his?"

"Then I may consider saving our marriage, but only if it's not his child." Unable to believe that Tammy had called her house, she shook her head with loathing. "I'm going to talk with Jordan."

Autumn was in the den when Lacy and Jordan arrived. "It's Friday, and I'm all packed to go back to my apartment." It had been a long week, and Autumn was ready to go home and take care of herself. She needed to be alone and had so much to think about.

"Do you have to go home today, Aunt Autumn?" Jordan asked.

"Yes, Sweetheart. I have to go home."

"I wish you would stay another week. I hate being here alone," Lacy said in disappointment. "How can you leave me at a time like this? My marriage is gone to hell."

"You need time alone just as I do. I have to put some perspective in my life. Right now I walk around like a zombie with no direction. Girl, you need to be alone with your son, and think about what you're going to do about your marriage." Autumn watched Jordan as he ran into the kitchen. She heard the refrigerator door open and close.

"What damn marriage? He may have that woman pregnant. Frankly, I don't know what he saw in her in the first place. Her clothes look cheap, and it looks as though she hasn't been to a beauty salon ever. I thought Eric had better taste in women, especially after he married me."

"Yes, I'm sure you won't see what he saw in her." Looking at Lacy, Autumn felt sorry for her. She was the first person that she felt sorry for since the night she was beaten. Lacy's arrogance was pricking at her skin.

"I thought that I could help you, but now I'm depending on you like you haven't got any problems of your own," Lacy said.

"'Problems' doesn't begin to describe what I have to deal with, and my heart is still broken over Matthew. But I can accept the fact that I was wrong. I should have told him instead of building our relationship on a lie. One thing came out of the beating and losing Matthew, I have no urge for sex. And I spoke with Mom last night. She is going to try and convince Dad to attend a meeting with her."

"That will be the day," Lacy replied. "He doesn't understand the illness."

"I know, but I'm hoping and praying anyway. He's a God-fearing man, so he may change his mind."

The sisters hugged, and Autumn picked up her bag. Lacy followed her out the door. Autumn was going home to recapture her old life.

Chapter 8

Autumn was glad to be back in her apartment, but she was nervous about her first meeting. Betty would be attending it with her, and Autumn was certain that Emmit would conveniently have a headache. Lacy had never gone because she was afraid the room would be filled with perverts and losers. The room was always filled with teachers, lawyers, doctors, and other professionals as well. Autumn was relieved that Lacy didn't come; she would only make her feel worse about her recovery. She looked at the clock and dressed to go to her meeting.

About the time Autumn and Betty entered the room, Autumn became depressed that she would have to share her life story all over again with strangers. She and Betty sat in two empty chairs that were in a circle with the others. Just as she had known, Lacy and Emmit were no-shows.

When it was Autumn's turn to speak she hesitated as she glanced into the strange faces and felt Betty's hand on her arm for reassurance. Once Autumn started talking, she couldn't stop. Amid deep sobs, she talked of her abuse as a child and the compulsiveness she felt for sex. She explained how powerless she was over her sexual impulses. But now she was ready to reclaim her life as it once was. Being abandoned by Matthew and shamed in front of her father only made her more determined to get well. But Autumn did it not only for them; she wanted a normal life that she could live with dignity and clarity.

A month had flown by since Autumn had started her meetings and counseling. She had even planned to start teaching again the following week. She was healing well, and makeup hid the bruises on her face.

That morning, Autumn had woken up with a start. "HIV, Lord, I need to be tested for HIV today," she said out loud to herself. Why hadn't she thought of it before? She had always been so careful, but there wasn't anything she could do about being raped. Her heart pounded rapidly and the hairs on her arms shot straight up. She jumped out of bed and grabbed the phone. But then she remembered the doctor said that an HIV test had been performed while she was in the hospital. Autumn lay back on the pillow and relaxed. But she needed to see her doctor anyway. She wanted to be tested a second time, and she needed a written excuse for work when she returned the following week. For two days she'd felt as though she had had the flu. She dialed the number and was told that her doctor could see her that afternoon.

Autumn ambled to the bathroom and showered. It felt good to be back in her apartment. She wanted to be alone and not worry about Emmit looking at her as though he didn't recognize her or the sarcastic remarks that Lacy made about her illness. Autumn had been monitoring her phone calls, hoping Matthew would call, but somehow she knew he wouldn't. She was an embarrassment to him.

Autumn arrived at the doctor's office and followed the nurse to Room 3.

"You can place your purse on the chair so I can weigh you." Autumn had lost so much weight that she had to look at the scale twice before she was sure that it was correct.

"Why are you here today, Miss Evans?" the nurse asked, looking concerned.

"I think that I may have a virus, and I've been off work and need a written excuse before I go back."

"Are you eating? You've lost lots of weight."

"I haven't had much of an appetite lately."

"Okay. The doctor should be in soon." The nurse looked at the chart again and exited the room.

Autumn was reading a pamphlet on diabetes when the doctor entered. She closed the pamphlet and placed it on her lap. Dr. Harrell stood in front of her and extended his hand.

"How are you feeling, Autumn? It's been more than a year since your last visit."

"I had been doing well, but I was attacked more than a month ago." She dropped her eyes, then continued. "I was attacked and raped, Dr. Harrell. I need to be tested for HIV a second time, to be convinced that I don't have it."

"That's clever—you should be tested. I'm so sorry. Was he arrested?"

"No, and I was hurt badly. Now I feel as though I have the flu."

"Or the result of a bad case of nerves," Dr. Harrell replied. "Have you been coughing?"

"No, I just have chills and my body aches all over, but it's better today. I need a written excuse to take to work on Monday."

"Okay. I'll examine you first and the nurse will take blood for your HIV test." He watched Autumn as he adjusted the plastic gloves on his hands. Then she remembered the man that was with Zack that night had worn plastic gloves. Her heart beat so fast that she almost passed out on the table.

Dr. Harrell saw the sweat forming on her forehead; her eyelids were closing and she reeled backward as though she would fall off the table. "Autumn, lie down slowly." Dr. Harrell wet a paper towel to place on her forehead. "Is that better?"

"Yes. It's better, thank you. I guess I do have a bad case of nerves."

"Here, let me take your temperature. Just lie still for a few minutes." He waited, noticing small bruises on the side of her face. As he looked at her chart, he noticed Autumn had lost fifteen pounds since her last visit. Even in her face, she had gotten thinner.

"Well, you don't seem to be running a temperature, which is good." He reached for his pad and wrote her out a prescription. "You need to rest and drink lots of fluids. The results of the HIV test should be in by Wednesday. Come back in a week if you are not feeling better." He touched her hand, and left her for the nurse.

The nurse came in right after the doctor left and took blood. After that, Autumn rushed out of the office and into the fresh air. The plastic gloves kept flashing in front of her face, the voices, the laughter. She ran to her car, locked the doors, and took deep breaths. After she was composed, she started her car and sped off.

Autumn parked her car in front of her apartment. As she got out of the car, she heard Betty calling her name. Betty had been waiting for Autumn to return home, and Autumn had been so preoccupied she hadn't noticed Betty's car. Autumn unlocked the apartment door and held it open for Betty.

"You rushed to the door like someone was chasing you. Are you all right?"

"No. I just left the doctor's office and have to go to the bathroom." Once Autumn closed the bathroom door behind her, she placed a cold towel against her forehead. Autumn sat on the toilet seat for five minutes before replacing the towel on the rack and going to join her mother in the living room.

Autumn sat in the chair opposite the sofa where Betty waited. "You look so serious, Mom. Are you okay?"

"I'm okay. But I'm a little worried about you, though you look a sight better than you did when you first got out of your car. Are you sure that you're feeling all right?"

"Yes. As a matter of fact, I just left the doctor's office. I'm going to work next week."

"Don't you think next week is a little soon?"

"No, Mom, if I stay in this apartment another week I'll go crazy. I need to heal, and to do that I need to start living again. Teaching is my life. Now, enough about me. How is Dad?"

"Working. I have never seen a retired man work

so many hours. He did say that he missed you when you left."

"I don't know how he missed me. He hardly saw me."

"You know he does everything his own way. Trust me, he'll be ringing your doorbell soon." But Betty didn't know what was going through Emmit's head. Their marriage hadn't been the same since he'd found out about Autumn's illness and that Betty had kept it a secret from him. They had never been so far apart. Since Emmit was only sixty-one, tall, dark, and still a good-looking man, he could very well meet another woman and get married again. Nonsense, she thought. He wouldn't leave her for another woman. But it hurt her all the same, since she knew he still looked good enough if he really wanted to remarry. He was still sleeping in the den. If only she could get him in their bed again, she could make him forgive her.

"I haven't talked to Lacy for three days. Are she and Eric talking again?" Autumn asked.

"Nope. No such luck. But he hurt her. I don't know why men hurt us. Eric was a fool for getting another woman pregnant, and Lacy is stubborn. But I hope she is sensible and tries to salvage her marriage."

Autumn looked at Betty. "What are you talking about, Mom?"

"I was just saying that you hear about men cheating on their wives so often. I hate it that it had to happen to my daughter. Anyway, I just dropped by on my way to see Eric. He needs to go back home to his wife and child."

"Mom, stay out of it. Lacy will be angry."

"Lacy won't know, and you don't tell her." Betty was standing in front of Autumn and pointed her finger as if she was chastising a child.

Autumn sighed and flew both hands up. "I give up. I won't tell Lacy, but you are making a mistake. I just hope it doesn't backfire on you. Have you talked to Matthew, too?"

"No, of course not. Now, I have to go."

Autumn watched Betty as she strutted out the door. At fifty-five, she still looked good; her skin was a walnut brown, she kept her hair dyed dark brown, and her eyelashes were long over dark eyes. Betty got to her car and turned around. "Are you going to church on Sunday? I don't think the children like that new Sunday school teacher."

"I don't know, Mom."

"You should, honey. You would feel much better if you went to church at a time that you really need the Lord."

"You're right. I'll pick you up for eight o'clock service." Autumn went back inside, and she knew that Betty had called Matthew. It would be too hard for her to stay out of her daughters' business. "Damn," Autumn said out loud. "Forgot to ask Mom if she could trim my hair on Saturday." She touched her hair. Need more than just a trim, she thought.

Chapter 9

Autumn arrived at school an hour earlier than usual. She needed to prepare assignments for her students. The principal followed her into the classroom.

"Autumn, it's so good to have you back. I've been so worried about you, and the parents and children constantly ask for you." The principal held out her arms and the two women hugged. Autumn was her favorite teacher.

"It's good to be back, Diane. I got so bored at home every day."

"Are you feeling all right? You can take all the time you need," Diane said as she looked at the fading bruises on Autumn's face. She had never seen Autumn so thin; she was too thin. She must have been hurt badly.

"I feel much better now, and I'm lucky to be here in one piece." She placed her purse on the desk and pulled out her doctor's excuse.

"I'm going to my office. Send one of the children if you need me. Oh, the Walker boy is back with us again. His mother requested that he be in your class."

"Good. He was a good student."

It was eight-fifteen; her students would be lining up and waiting for Autumn to come out and lead them inside the classroom. The Walker boy was the first student who saw her. All the students smiled when they saw Autumn approaching the line.

"Good morning, class. Is everyone ready to start a busy day?"

"Yes, Miss Evans."

"Okay, let's go inside." She smiled, feeling giddy inside, and wondered how she stayed away so long. Teaching was her joy, her life. All she wanted was to teach and be happy again. While walking back to her class, she thought of Matthew and felt as though she was sinking. But she had to take her mind off him. The children needed her undivided attention, and she needed theirs.

After the children had put away their lunches and settled in their seats, Autumn had each child tell her what he or she had learned while Autumn was away. The morning started off well, and the children worked until lunch with no interruptions.

At two-thirty the children were ready to leave and stood in a straight line so Autumn could lead them outside.

She stayed until four-thirty and got assignments ready for the next morning.

On her way home, she decided to stop in Albertson's market.

Autumn was tired and could feel it in her shoulders and ribs, but the doctor said it would take a while after going back to work. But that day she felt better than any day since leaving the hospital.

As Autumn got out of her car and started walking, she heard someone walking close behind her.

"Joan! Joan!"

Autumn kept walking. A man jumped in front of her. He was tall, about forty years old, with a light complexion and close-cut hair. She looked into his face, feeling completely disheveled. Instantly, she got an eerie feeling.

"Aren't you a teacher at Compton Elementary School?"

Autumn took a step backward. He was standing too close. "Yes. I do teach there. Are you the parent of one of my students?" She was beginning to feel at ease.

"Don't you even remember me? We met in a bar in Santa Monica. Or maybe you would remember that we went to the Wilshire Inn Hotel? Must I say more?"

She looked into his light-brown eyes as he stared at her. Again, she felt eerie. Then suddenly she remembered. He was the worse sex partner she had ever had, and all she'd wanted to do was forget they ever met. How could she not remember him? Autumn felt ill as she remembered that night. He was angry because she'd insisted that he wear a condom. He'd lost his erection before he could slip on the condom, then he'd pulled it off and tried another one. He'd damaged three condoms before they'd had sex, and it was over before Autumn realized they had started.

She felt disgusted by being in his presence again. "I remember you, but right now I'm in a hurry." She started to walk away when he grabbed her arm.

"Not so fast. We have some unfinished business to take care of."

Her fear was turning into anger, and she jerked her

arm from him. No man would ever force her to do anything she didn't want to again. She would fight to her death. "We have no unfinished business. Now leave me alone."

"I can always tell the principal of the school how we met. I wonder what she would have to say about you. You are a teacher; you should set an example for the children."

Autumn's heart leaped. She had played this nightmare over and over again in her head. But she wouldn't be bullied by anyone. She had paid her dues for the life she lived. "How did you know that I'm a teacher? I didn't tell you."

"I know. Don't worry about how I found out. You just follow me."

She couldn't imagine being locked in a room with him, or any other man since the beating. She felt ill, afraid, and saw Zack's face flash in front of her. His brother's laughter in her ears, and the punches to her ribs until she could barely breathe, and when she could breathe no longer she'd collapsed. Autumn felt she could no longer control herself and felt her life was in danger. She wouldn't be forced to go with him, and the anger in her was about to explode.

Greg smiled, then stopped when he saw her take another step back as though she would run.

"You filthy pig, you animal," she shouted. "Get away from me." She couldn't stop and yelled at the top of her voice. People were walking by and stopped to witness the fight.

Greg was shocked when she lifted her purse high and it came down hard on the side of his head.

"You will not force me," she yelled between closed teeth, waving her purse like a mad woman. "Never,

never will I do it again. You want a piece of me? Come on, you bastard, over my dead body." Autumn wanted him to come closer, and she wanted to kill this man. She wanted him to feel her pain, and beg her for forgiveness. But most of all, she wanted to kill him. "I'm going to carry a gun for trash like you." Her fist was balled, and the strap on her purse was wrapped around one hand.

"You crazy bitch."

Two large-built men stopped in front of Autumn. "Miss, are you okay?"

"You'll be sorry," Greg said, and rushed away from her.

"Miss, is there anything we can do?"

"No, no. Just leave me the fuck alone." She ran to her car, got in, and locked the doors. Autumn cried, beating her fists against the steering wheel. "Why! Why! Why!" she screamed. Five minutes later, she wiped her eyes. She was trembling so badly, she wasn't sure if she could drive home, but she did get home safely.

Once she was inside, she checked all the windows and doors to make sure they were locked.

Autumn lay across her bed, pressing a wet, cold towel against her forehead, and wondered how she'd gotten home without having an accident. She didn't remember stopping at any red lights or stop signs.

Chapter 10

Autumn took the towel from her forehead and rushed into the bathroom. She fell to her knees, vomiting into the toilet. She was still tense, and her stomach was doing somersaults and her head pounded. She changed into her pajamas and opened a 7-Up. Back in her bedroom, she grabbed the remote, got into bed, and flipped on the television. She stayed inside all day Saturday.

Sunday morning Autumn was up early and dressed. "I'm glad you're coming with me to church this morning, honey," Betty said as Autumn drove. "I tried to convince Lacy to go with us, but she said maybe next Sunday. She's having a pretty hard time right now." Betty watched Autumn as she nodded absentmindedly. "Are you all right, Autumn?"

"Yeah, Mom. I heard everything you said. I've had a lot on my mind lately." They were going to the eight o'clock service, and Autumn couldn't get there fast enough.

"Are you staying to teach Sunday school today?"

"No, not today," Autumn answered. "I'm not ready

yet." After the incident in Albertson's parking lot with Greg, she still wasn't feeling well. Maybe she wasn't ready to go back to work so soon after all. But staying at home feeling sorry for herself was worse. She just wished that she wasn't so afraid all the time, and around everyone, especially men.

Betty had wanted to ask her a question but didn't know how. If she wanted an answer, then she had to ask. "Autumn?"

"Yes, Mom?"

For a few seconds, Betty hesitated. "Are you having any sexual desires? I don't mean the normal kind. Well, you know what I'm asking."

Autumn felt ashamed, but had to answer. "I know what you're asking, and the answer is no. I don't think that I will desire sex ever again."

"You will, but with a man that you are in love with and one who loves you. It's just too soon after that bad experience you've had."

Autumn turned the corner and parked in front of the church.

"Come on, Autumn. There are empty seats in the middle row."

As Autumn walked behind Betty, she admired the wide black hat her mother was wearing. Betty had seemed excited to have Autumn come with her to church today.

Autumn listened closely as the choir sang her favorite song, hoping to feel her spirit lift, and waiting to hear a word, a sentence—anything—to make her feel alive again.

Finally, Reverend Jones asked if he could say a prayer for those who needed it. People started walking to the front of the church. Reluctantly, Autumn got up and Betty gladly followed. They were on their knees, and Autumn prayed with all her heart and soul.

It was nine-thirty, and the service was over. Autumn and Betty were walking out the door when she saw Cory Walker, her student who'd transferred to another school and had returned.

Cory looked up at Autumn with a wide smile as he saw her coming closer.

"Hi, Cory," Autumn spoke and smiled down at the little boy.

"Hi, Miss Evans."

"Hello, Mrs. Walker." Autumn extended her hand. "It was a pleasure to see that Cory had returned when I got back from my leave of absence. I don't think that I've ever seen you here before."

"This is my third Sunday. I requested that Cory be placed in your classroom. He loves you so much, Miss Evans."

"I was happy to see Cory. Oh, this is my mother, Betty Smith."

"Daddy, Miss Evans is here."

The gentleman turned around to face Autumn, and extended his hand.

The words were stuck in Autumn's throat and stayed there. She couldn't speak and instantly took a step backward. His hand was still extended, but Autumn purposely ignored it.

"Hello. I'm Greg Walker, Cory's father."

Autumn took a deep breath and decided that she wouldn't let him know that he could intimidate her. She would play his little game, and he would find out who he was messing with.

"It's good to finally meet you, Mr. Walker. You were never present for the parent and teacher meetings. I've often wondered where the other parent was when only one would show up. Do you work nights, Mr. Walker?"

Greg cleared his throat. "No, and I'm sorry. But I work overtime some evenings."

"Overtime? I understand perfectly," she said sarcastically. "You know, your face looks familiar. Have I seen you somewhere?"

Greg cleared his throat again. "I don't think so," he answered dryly.

"Anyway, if there are ever any concerns about Cory, please let me know. I'm sure the three of us can find a lot to talk about," Autumn said looking at Mr. and Mrs. Walker. "Wouldn't you agree, Mr. Walker?" She looked at Greg and smiled. "I always tell my students' parents that I never know how much I can find out until I speak with both parents, about everything." With a warning, she looked straight into Greg's eyes.

"We really appreciate you taking this time with us, Miss Evans," Mrs. Walker said. "That's why all the children love you so much."

"Thank you. And Mr. Walker, it was nice meeting you. I'm not worried about Cory. He's one of my best students." She watched the frown on Greg's face and smiled.

"Are you ready, Mom?"

Autumn watched as Mr. and Mrs. Walker walked in front of her. He kept his distance and didn't turn around to look at her.

Autumn knew that she didn't have to worry about Greg any longer. She knew where he worked, and where he lived. All she had to do was look in Cory's file.

Autumn drove Betty home. "Why don't you come in, Autumn. I'll cook breakfast."

"Mom, I really don't feel well. I've had an upset stomach all week." She couldn't tell Betty her upset stomach started the day she was in the parking lot with Greg.

"Well, I guess I'll have to eat alone."

"Why? Where's Dad?"

"He got up early this morning and went to get his car washed so he could go to the racetracks with some guys from his job."

"Why didn't you go with him?" Autumn asked curiously. What was going on with her parents, she wondered.

"I don't like racetracks. Besides, it's Sunday and I wanted to go to church, and I'm glad that I did. It gave you a chance to pray in the house of the Lord."

"Okay. I'll have breakfast. Maybe it will make me feel better." Autumn waited until they were inside. "Mom, are you and Dad still having problems because of me?"

"No, honey. We're having problems like any couple that has been married for a long time. Couples grow cold then hot again. Now, don't worry. I'm going to change clothes so I can cook. I'm starving." Betty went to her room and sat on the edge of the bed and sighed. She didn't know what kind of phase her marriage was going through and was worried about it.

Autumn waited in the den and looked through the current *Ebony* magazine. She read a short article and closed the magazine. Sundays her parents went to church together. What was so important at the track that her father couldn't spend the entire weekend with Betty like he used to? Lately, when Autumn called her parents' house, it seemed like Emmit was never home.

Betty went into the kitchen and cooked eggs, grits, and bacon.

Autumn poured two cups of coffee and placed them on the table. She remembered when she was younger and used to help Betty cook in this kitchen or did her homework at the table while Betty cooked.

Autumn watched Betty as she took her seat at the table. "Mom, I read a book once that said Dad is at a dangerous age. Maybe you should do more of what he likes. You really should be with him right now."

"Autumn, I know Emmit. He'll come around soon. And even if he is at some dangerous age, we've been married too long for him to do anything foolish about it. Now eat your breakfast before it gets cold."

For a while, they made idle conversation. But Autumn had to try again.

"I can't stop worrying about you and Dad. He's only sixty-one, and he's still a handsome man. Maybe you should consider that, Mom. People get divorced after forty years of marriage. I hate to see that happen to you."

"Autumn, we're not getting a divorce. Your dad and I are creatures of habit. We have our little cold spells. After it's over, he'll say, 'Betty, let's go to church and brunch.' Everything will be the same as usual. You just stop worrying and get better."

"I can't stop worrying because it started when he found out about me. In a way it's my fault."

Betty watched Autumn as she wiped a tear with her napkin. "No, it started before that. It's not your problem, honey. Me and Emmit will work it through like we always have."

Autumn placed the dishes in the dishwasher while Betty cleared the table. "I'm glad I ate. Now, I'm going home and read a new novel. But remember what I said, Mom."

Betty kissed Autumn on the cheek and walked her outside. She admired the mint-green pantsuit and short waist jacket that Autumn was wearing; Autumn's hair was up in back. She looked lovely, even though she was still too thin.

On Autumn's way home, she decided to stop by Lacy's house. They hadn't talked in three days, and Lacy had sounded depressed. Autumn parked her car; Eric was backing out of the driveway, fast. He hadn't even noticed her.

Autumn rang the doorbell four times before Lacy swung open the door.

"What? Oh, it's you." She turned and stepped away so Autumn could pass.

"Hello to you, too." Autumn closed the door and went inside. "Where's Jordan?"

"He went to Disneyland with the little boy who lives across the street, thank goodness." Lacy sat on the sofa, placing both hands against her eyes, and sobbed. "It is getting worse between me and Eric, and I don't know what to do about it. Today we had an awful argument. I mean it got real ugly. He had the nerve to say it was my fault. He was sleeping around, but it's my fault."

Autumn shook her head. "So what do you want to do, Lacy? You're unhappy, and Jordan misses his father. If the baby is Eric's, then you'll have to decide if you can forgive him and accept his baby."

"I can't accept the baby. That stupid, common-looking woman will call here every day if the baby is his. I won't tolerate it, and Eric and I would end up getting a divorce anyway. If it happens, I will sue his pants off. He'll have nothing left to give her or the baby. I won't forget what he's done to me. Anyway, I asked him to wait until the baby was born, so we could find out if it's his, before he moves back in here." Lacy sniffed and held her head high.

"He should give you anything you ask for. After all, he's at fault. I went to church with Mom this morning, but Dad wasn't home. He went to the race-track with some men from his job."

"Racetrack my ass." Lacy leaped off the sofa. "I saw him and another woman at the Howard Johnson Theater last night, but he didn't see me. He's probably with her right now."

"You went to see a movie?"

"No. I went to the bookstore. Jordon wasn't home and I needed to get out of the house."

Autumn didn't understand how Lacy could have such a conversation about their parents without showing any emotions at all. Didn't it mean anything to her that Emmit was cheating, and their mother was sitting home alone? "Did you confront him about it? They are our parents, Lacy. Do you even care?"

"To be honest, no I don't care and I didn't want to look at him or the woman. I have problems of my own, and so do you." Lacy flopped back down on the sofa and crossed her legs, then rolled her eyes.

"I don't believe you, Lacy. You only think of yourself."

"You're damn right I do. Mom gets into our business and gives Dad orders like he's her child instead of her husband. When was the last time she treated him like her partner? And I'm not telling her anything about the woman. Let her figure it out for herself. I need a Pepsi; want one?" she asked matter-of-factly.

Autumn shook her head at Lacy's cool demeanor regarding their parents. "Yes, I guess so."

"Okay. Now we can get back to my problem. That's what's important here." She sauntered to the kitchen, and Autumn sat back in the chair and closed her eyes, waiting for Lacy's return.

"Here's your Pepsi. Are you feeling better these days?"

"Yes. But right now I'm worried about Mom. Do you think Dad will leave her?"

"I'm sure that I don't know, Autumn, and my life is upside down. How can I concentrate on them when I can't get my own life on track?"

"You are right. How can you concentrate on your life and theirs, too?" As Autumn thought of it, Lacy was right. She had her own crisis, and it was catastrophic enough to figure out her own life. There wasn't anything that she could say to make Lacy feel better, so Autumn decided to go home and correct some school papers.

As she drove home, she thought of her father with another woman. How could she tell Betty to wake up and concentrate on her marriage? Was it right for her to tell her mother about the other woman? No, she would first speak to her father. Betty was still an attractive woman, with hardly any wrinkles in her face; maybe her body had more curves, but she still looked nice.

Getting out of the car, Autumn took deep breaths

but felt weak. She was afraid that she was going to throw up before she got inside her apartment, but the feeling quickly evaporated as she rushed inside. Lately, every time was got disconcerted, she felt ill.

"Emmit, where have you been? It is ten o'clock, and you've been gone all day. You're always home early on Sundays," Betty said in a displeasing tone. She had been waiting in the den for him. Betty got up from the sofa and pulled the belt tightly around her bathrobe. She was standing in her bare feet and slipped on her slippers.

"Woman, don't grill me before I can walk into the house." Emmit walked past her, and Betty flip-flopped behind him. She'd waited up for him so they could talk. The strain between them was getting to be agonizing, and from the conversation earlier with Autumn, Betty knew that she had to be proactive about her marriage. "I'm talking to you, Emmit."

He hung his jacket inside the closet and turned around to face her but didn't answer.

"Emmit, I won't live like this. You walk around with a chip on your shoulder. I've apologized over and over about keeping Autumn's condition a secret, and when our daughters need us most, you bail out on them." She flopped down hard on the bed, her arms folded against her chest.

Emmit couldn't look in her eyes; he started to undress. All he wanted was to sleep and think of the nice, loving day he'd spent. There were no complaints, no quarreling, no one telling him what to do. He was a man and needed some attention. He was genuinely sorry about the problems in their daughters' lives, but they were adults, and their problems were theirs. He couldn't undo them.

"I needed some time to myself, Betty. You fuss too much, and you don't include me in anything."

Betty's intake of breath sounded like a hiss. "What are you talking about? All the years that you were in the service I had to make decisions for our family. You weren't here then, but you are now. We seem to be going in a different direction. We're not together anymore, Emmit." She couldn't believe that he had waltzed in here and expected her to say nothing to him.

"That was your choice, not mine." He didn't wait for her to answer and went into the bathroom, then walked out wearing his pajamas. He grabbed a pillow off the bed. "I'm sleeping on the sofa in the den. Good night, Betty." He stopped at the bedroom door with his back to her. "Next weekend, I'm moving out." He went to the den, turned out the light, and lay down on the sofa.

Betty was stung, her mouth was open; seconds passed before she could speak again. What had happened to their lives, their family? No, she wouldn't accept this; she wouldn't lose her husband. Betty got up and went to the den.

Emmit had just gotten into a comfortable position when the lights came on. He opened one eye, waiting for Betty to speak.

"Have you lost your mind? What do you mean, you're moving out?" She had to fight, and for the first time since they were married, her marriage was in a serious dilemma. She watched him sit up, and she sat next to him. "Emmit, what do you mean that you're moving out? You couldn't be serious."

"Yes, I'm serious. I'm tired, Betty, and I'm tired of being treated secondhand. I heard you three nights ago arguing on the phone with Matthew. I told you to stay the hell out of it. Then you turned around and called Eric for the second time. Nothing I say seems to matter."

"You have to understand that I raised the girls up by myself."

"They weren't that old when I retired from the Air Force, so you didn't raise them completely by yourself."

"But they came to me when they had a problem. Still, I was always thankful for being married to you, and some times I was lonely, but I was true to you. Moving out is the worst mistake you could make. I want to work it out, and I'm willing to change some of my ways." She moved closer to him. "Give it more time, Emmit."

"I'm not entirely sure that you can change, Betty, and I don't want to spend another year of my life in a dead marriage."

"But, Emmit. If you still love me you would give me another chance. Let me prove to you that I can be a dedicated wife." She had made up her mind that she would plead, beg, do whatever she had to do to keep her husband. Betty looked at Emmit as he lay still on the sofa. He looked so good, and sexy. He was a big strong man.

"I'm tired, Betty, and I need more time to think about it. But take my warning seriously." He turned his back to her.

Betty watched Emmit for a few seconds longer when she decided to trample back to the bedroom. She knew how relentless he was. If he didn't want to talk he wouldn't, and right now wasn't the time to force it.

"June, we've been married too many years for me to just walk out and not give Betty another chance. Maybe she was right about me bailing out on my daughters when they needed me most. This is something that I have to do."

June was disenchanted with his explanation. "I was under the impression that we would really get together, but no, you have to go back to your wife. I guess I deserve the disappointment for screwing around with a married man." She had tried to be understanding, but now her dreams had fallen apart.

"It's not what you think, honey. I do love you, June. But with the problems that my daughters are having, now isn't a good time for me to leave my family." Emmit and June were lying in bed. He pulled her into his arms and held her close.

Five years earlier, Emmit and Betty had met June at a party. She was charming, and easy to talk to. Five months ago, she and Emmit had run into each other at CVS Pharmacy in El Segundo. Emmit was on his way home and stopped to buy some cough drops for Betty. He watched June as she walked out of the store, then remembered where they had met. She smiled up at him, and before he left she gave him her phone number. When Emmit got to his car, he started to toss the number on the ground, but he'd kept it. He knew then that he had made a mistake. June was a woman that a man couldn't get out his head. Emmit, feeling that he didn't mean anything to Betty, got lonely and called June. Their relationship flourished in weeks. Now he loved her. It was painful to leave her.

June was a fifty-one-year-old with a twenty-five-year-old's body. She enjoyed the sex with Emmit, loved to see him smile, and was attentive in every way. She wouldn't even answer her phone when they were together. Emmit asked for so little, it was hard for any woman to stop loving him. She would miss him desperately.

Emmit rose up on one elbow and looked into June's eyes. She was in just as much pain as he. For the first time in years, he had a woman who gave him attention, made love with him every time they were together. Their relationship was so easy to get attached to. He would miss slipping his hand under her dress and feeling her soft hips and having her love it. She wore only short nightgowns when they were together, and he would be in his clothes for only five minutes after his arrival. June was a full-size woman, with hips the size that Emmit loved. Her hair was black and wavy and she had dark eyes and smooth, dark skin.

"I can't stand the thought of being without you, Emmit. What am I going to do?" she whispered, then kissed his neck, which was always a turn-on for him. She held her breath to prevent herself from crying. She couldn't let him see her cry. After all, he was going back to his wife. She closed her eyes and imagined him making love to Betty, but just as fast she forced the vision out of her head. Right now he was with her and whether Emmit knew it or not, he would come back to her again. He was like a hungry man without food. He had gone too long without having a woman to love him and give him what he needed.

"Leaving you is killing me. I better go before I get on top of you again. With you, I can't seem to get enough." He slowly got out of bed and dressed. She lay back down and saw the hunger in his eyes as he looked down at her.

June then got up and walked Emmit to the door. "I'll always love you," Emmit whispered against her ear.

"The night-light will always be burning for you, just as my heart will." She let go as he pulled loose and walked out the door.

As Emmit drove home, he felt as though he would never be happy again, but he owed it to Betty to at least try and make their marriage work. He had never seen her so afraid, and she needed him. For the first time in their marriage, she'd actually said she needed him. But the fact still remained that he loved June. He would try and forget the hours they made love: her eyes that blazed with fire when he touched her, the sweetness of her kisses, the beauty of her face and soft skin, and the hours that he'd held her in his arms listening to the quietness around them. She was a warm, extraordinary woman.

Emmit placed the key in the door, and the warm fragrance from the kitchen made him realize how hungry he was.

"Ready for dinner?" Betty asked.

"Yes. I'm starving, and it smells great. I've missed your cooking, Betty."

She smiled in anticipation of the new start in their marriage. She knew that the last few weeks with Autumn and Lacy's problems had been a strain in their marriage. But Emmit didn't understand that she had to help their daughters get their lives in order. Eric hadn't returned any of her phone calls, and Matthew had asked her to never call him again. She was only trying to get him and Autumn back together again. But it wasn't too late for Lacy and Eric. She had to speak to him before Lacy filed for a divorce.

As Autumn walked down the long aisle in the supermarket, she kept seeing the same man who had walked into the store behind her. Was he following her? Did he recognize her as a one-night sex instrument? She didn't recognize him and was too frightened to study his face. In her meetings, she was told to expect running into one of her partners, but she dreaded it. She couldn't go through another experience like she'd had with Greg. But she would not be intimidated either. When would it all end? In an instant, she felt ill and afraid, and she left the basket of food in the middle of the aisle.

She hurried to her car and locked the door. She looked outside, but he didn't follow her. She hastily drove out of the parking lot.

Darkness had fallen by the time Autumn arrived home. Lately, she'd been rushing inside, locking the door, and checking all the windows. Still traumatized, she lay across the bed in silence, listening for any movements.

The next morning, Autumn woke up at five. Her stomach cramped, and both temples ached. She got out of bed and saw a large blood stain on her light blue sheet. Autumn went to the bathroom; feeling weak, she sat on the toilet. She felt a blood clot force its way out of her and fall into the toilet. She groaned and frowned, and instantly became panicky as the cramps worsened. She got dressed and drove to the hospital.

She was thankful that only one person was in the emergency room ahead of her. While she was being admitted, she felt another cramp and doubled over.

"Can you stand?" the nurse asked with concern.

"It hurts more than any cramps I've had, and I feel as though I'm going to faint." Autumn felt beads of sweat across her forehead.

The nurse rushed around the counter and grabbed Autumn's arm. "Here, I'm taking you to a bed."

Relieved, Autumn waddled slowly, and the nurse stopped at the first partition and helped her lie down. "Here, lie down for a while, and I'll get you a gown to slip on." She left Autumn for fifteen minutes and returned with a white gown.

"Leave the back open." The nurse left Autumn alone again, and a young doctor came in to examine her. Autumn closed her eyes and pretended she wasn't there.

The doctor was young, and quiet. "I have some bad news, Miss Evans."

"What?" Autumn asked. What on earth could he have found wrong from a simple examination? But he looked serious.

"You lost the baby. It looks like you were probably about two months along."

"Baby?" She sat up quickly, moaned, and placed one hand against her stomach. "What do you mean baby?" She looked shocked, then remembered she hadn't had her period since she came home from the hospital. She'd thought it was because of the terrible beating, and hadn't thought anything of it—especially about having a baby.

"You didn't know?"

"No, doctor. I didn't know. Can you give me something for the pain, and I will go home."

He looked at her strangely. "Maybe you should stay overnight."

"Thanks, but I've seen enough of hospitals to last me for the rest of my life."

"Okay. I have something that you can take now. Lie down for a while. Tomorrow, call your doctor if you have any more pain or heavy bleeding. The nurse will bring the medication in shortly." He walked out, shook his head, and went to his next patient.

"Pregnant," she said out loud. She felt lucky that she had lost it. To bring a child into this world after what had happened to her would be her retribution for a lifetime. No. No way on earth would she have a baby for the two monsters who harmed her. She dressed quickly, pulling her sweater over her head, and slipped into her shoes at the same time. Autumn didn't wait for the nurse; instead she rushed out of the room and ran to the elevator. When she reached her car she drove fast out of the parking lot, as though someone was chasing her. "No, no, no," she screamed.

It was eight-thirty in the morning when Autumn arrived back at her apartment and left a message for the principal. As much as she hated to admit it, there was no way that she could teach that day. She remembered the medication that Matthew left when he had knee surgery. She went to the bathroom and popped the top off the bottle and took two of the pills. It made her quickly fall into a deep slumber.

Autumn thought she was dreaming when she heard the doorbell ringing. Still feeling the effects of the medication, she slowly crawled out of bed.

"I called the school and was told you were ill. Didn't you hear the phone? I called you twice." Lacy asked, and then noticed Autumn was still in her pajamas. She walked right past her to the living room.

"I didn't hear anything." Autumn closed the door and locked it. "I felt horrible today." She flopped down in the chair and curled her feet under her, running her fingers through her hair. "I'm not a sight for sore eyes I know. I had a miscarriage," she said as matter-a-factly as she could.

"You what?"

Autumn rested her head back on the chair. "You heard right. I didn't even know that I was pregnant. Sometimes, I think I'm losing my mind."

"You've been through too much to have noticed. Did you want the child?"

"No. No way I would have had the child. Oh God, Lacy. I feel like a different person. I don't feel like I'm living anymore." She placed both hands to her eyes and cried softly.

Lacy felt sorry for her. "I know how you feel, Autumn. I feel as though I'm sleepwalking." Lacy stood up. "I better go back to my office and see what is waiting for me. But first I had to see if you were all right. You should go back to bed. Gee, you look terrible."

"Thanks." Autumn stood up and walked Lacy to the door. "Have you talked to Eric lately?"

"Not for a week, but he'll pick up Jordan on Saturday. There isn't anything to talk about until the baby is born. If it's his, I'll divorce him." Lacy stopped at the door. "I visited Mom yesterday. Dad was home, and she was happy. But you know, it didn't seem like much had changed. She was on the phone with Miss Berger talking about the woman across the street with four kids by four different men. You would think she would give Dad more attention. You better go back to bed. Gee, you really do look lousy. Isn't it time you got your life back to normal?"

"I just had a miscarriage, Lacy. Give me a break." Autumn slammed the door before Lacy could respond.

Autumn went back to bed, but now she was too upset to sleep. Two days later, she was still in bed. She was sinking into an exhausted depression and was having difficulty pulling herself out of it. On the third day, she went to her meeting and listened to new members who were worse off than she was. There was a young woman who had gone to a motel with a man and was gang-raped. Autumn cried all the way home.

Once she got home, she knew that she had to find a will to go forward with her life. She was still alive, breathing, and lucky, considering what could have happened to her. But as she thought about it, she could remember what it felt like to be happy again. She was still unhappy over her father's cool politeness, though. Just to think that he felt differently about her was like a knife going through her chest.

After four days, Autumn decided to go back to work. Her classroom was where she belonged, but the void in her heart and the loss of Matthew was eating away at her.

After work she arrived at her apartment, alone, where she would lose her appetite and feel depressed. The memory of the night she was abused would float back. Being alone gave her the chance to think too much.

Finally, Autumn had gotten through another week.

That Friday, she called Alma, her sponsor, who also attended the meetings. Alma was forty and had been attending the meetings for four years without going back to her old habits.

"Think positive, Autumn. What you're going through now, we all have. But I was lucky. I wasn't abused like you were. Do everything that will help you to forget that night. If you can't forgive yourself, then how can anyone else forgive you? It shows when you live with all that grievance and distrust. It only brings more negativity into your life and thoughts. Have you had cravings for any sexual activity lately?"

"No, not at all. The way I feel now, I think even when I meet the right man, I may not want to have sex with him. Just the thought of that night turns off all sexual arousal for me."

"You only feel this way because you are afraid and don't trust yourself or anyone else. But give it more time. You can call me anytime you need to talk. If you like, we can meet some place and have coffee."

"Thank you, Alma. You've been some help to me. I'll remember your advice."

As soon as Autumn hung up the phone it rang again and she picked up.

"Hi, honey. I haven't talked to you in two days. Are you all right?" Betty asked.

"I'm all right, so don't worry so much about me, Mom."

"You don't sound all right. Lacy said that you haven't been feeling well."

"I guess she told you what happened." Leave it to Lacy, Autumn thought.

"Yes, honey. She told me, and I'm sorry. Autumn,

why don't you go to church tonight instead of staying at home alone. It may make you feel better. I always tell Lacy to go, but she doesn't listen to anything I tell her. Just go and see if it lifts your spirit. God is the only person that can help you."

"I'm tired, Mom, but if I feel better I may go. How's Dad?"

"He's well. We're going to a movie tonight. Now remember what I said. Go to church. Trust me, you'll feel better."

All Autumn wanted to do was crawl into bed and cover her head. She hadn't gone out of her apartment after dark since she left the hospital. It had been a week since she ate dinner, and tonight was no different. She ate a peanut butter and jelly sandwich and called it a meal.

Autumn went to her bedroom and flipped on the TV with the remote control so she could watch the news. She changed the channels, but nothing interested her. After lying across her bed for half an hour, she decided to go to church. She would try anything to help herself forget the past, or learn to live with it.

Autumn changed into a pair of navy slacks and matching sweater, combed her hair, and ambled out the door.

She strode brusquely into the sanctuary and was pleasantly surprised to see every seat was filled. There was a concert going on. The usher seated her in the middle row, beside a gentleman who smiled and nodded as she sat down next to him. She looked straight ahead and tried to relax. But she felt safe inside the church, and the words to the song were so meaningful, as though the song was meant only for her. People stood up and sang along with the choir.

Autumn had forgotten her problems and had even smiled at the gentlemen next to her.

By ten, the concert was over, and as Autumn walked to the parking lot she spoke to two women who were members of the church. Then she saw the gentlemen who'd sat next to her during the concert walking beside her. He smiled and nodded, and she watched him as he got inside his car and drove off.

Once Autumn was home, she changed into her pajamas. She had to admit Betty had been right; going to church was better than staying home and feeling sorry for herself. She was in her bedroom and stood in front of the mirror. What happened to her happy smile, the glint in her eyes, and the woman who loved life and wasn't afraid of anything? She had turned into an angry, frightened stranger. It was time to make a change in her life. She had made mistakes and had paid dearly for them. She had lost the man she loved and had planned to spend her life with, and in the midst of it she had lost herself. She had to find a way to take control of her life again.

A year ago, Autumn had bought a book that would help her understand sex addiction. She went to her bookcase and stood there for a few seconds, her hand trembling as she reached for it. She went to the kitchen and made a pot of coffee to keep herself awake. Autumn would read all night, and with every fiber of her being, she would understand and reclaim her life.

At five the next morning, Autumn couldn't keep her eyes open any longer. She fell asleep with the book open across her chest. But when she woke up at 10:00 AM, she knew that reading the book was well worth it. Finally, she had answers to her unanswered questions.

Autumn showered, and for the first time in months she cooked a well-balanced breakfast. After breakfast, she dressed and went shopping for clothes and food.

Chapter 11

"My, you look pretty, Autumn," Betty said and stood back so Autumn could come inside the house. Autumn was wearing purple jeans and a sweater. Betty looked at her face and saw that the bruises had almost disappeared. She looked beautiful with her hair combed away from her face. She looked young and radiant again.

"Emmit, Autumn is here," Betty yelled from the living room.

Emmit walked in and pulled his daughter into his arms. They sat in the living room, and Autumn sat on the sofa next to him. "What brings you this way, daughter?"

"I just finished shopping and wanted to see my parents, that's all. Also, I wanted to say that I'm sorry for all the worry I've caused. I'm trying to find my way back to my real life again."

Emmit grabbed her hand and held it in his. "You'll be all right, Autumn. You've always been strong, and we're here to help you."

"Thanks, Dad." She looked at Betty. "Mom, please don't cry."

"I can't help it. I just want my daughters to be happy."

The doorbell rang and Autumn answered it. To her surprise, it was Eric. He took one step inside and hesitated when he saw Emmit. Betty spoke but Emmit didn't.

"I was in the neighborhood and thought I would stop by and say hello," Eric blurted out. He hadn't seen Emmit's car parked in the driveway and had assumed he wasn't home.

Autumn watched her father, but he still hadn't said anything to Eric. Instead, he looked angry, his chin set stubbornly, and he sat up straight on the sofa.

"Betty, I'm sorry that I didn't have time to talk when you called me at work last week. But it had gotten hectic at the office."

Autumn and Emmit looked at Betty, then at each other.

"Now, look. I just wanted to tell you the same thing I told Lacy. You two have a son who doesn't understand why his mama and daddy are living in separate places." She shook her head in frustration as she tried to ignore Emmit's accusing stares.

"Betty, I think that you should leave that up to Eric and Lacy. After all he did get another woman pregnant. I say he's lucky if Lacy took him back at all," Emmit said with honest bluntness. He looked at Eric and saw his discomfort.

"I know that I made a grave mistake, but I will do whatever it takes to make Lacy forgive me."

"Just don't ask for my help," Emmit said.

"Emmit, Eric needs to get his family back, and I want to see them back together again, too."

"Then let him try. And while he's trying, he should keep his pants zipped."

Emmit got up and went to the den.

"Are you all right, Autumn?" Eric asked.

"Yes. I'm well. Eric, I have to be honest. I don't approve of what you've done, but if Lacy is willing to take you back, then I'll wish you two luck."

"That's all I can ask from her family." He stood up and took a quick glance at his watch. "I'm picking up my son, so I better leave now."

Betty walked him to the door. When she took her seat again, she saw the look of disapproval on Autumn's face and wondered what Emmit would say to her when Autumn left.

"Does Lacy know you've been calling Eric?"

"No. She doesn't know. But why shouldn't I call him? He's my son-in-law."

"Don't you think that they can work out their own problems, Mom? And don't ever call Matthew again, either. I don't appreciate it."

"Look, Autumn—"

Autumn held up one hand to stop her. "No, Mom. I mean it. Don't call him again. He's out of my life. If he wanted me back, he wouldn't need help from you."

"I'm just trying to help my daughters."

"You try and help your marriage, and let us take care of our business." Autumn stood and picked up her purse off the sofa, then started to the door.

"Wait a minute. There's nothing wrong in my marriage. What are you talking about, Autumn?"

"Dad was gone for a while. Now he's back, and you assume there's nothing wrong in your marriage?"

"That was then, this is now. We are getting along well."

"Wake up, Mom. I don't see that anything has changed. But I hope so for your sakes." She started to walk out, but turned to face Betty. "Lacy is going to have a fit when she finds out that you've called Eric." Autumn rushed out the door. It was hard to know if her father was happy or not, but at least he was happy to see her. Maybe their relationship could be as good as it used to be. Maybe, she thought.

It was Sunday morning, and Autumn was getting dressed to go to church. She was in a happy mood and felt good about doing all the things she liked most.

She went to the kitchen and placed the empty coffee cup in the sink, grabbed her keys from the counter, and sauntered out the door.

The church was crowded and the new pastor had arrived. Autumn saw two seats in the middle row and sat down. It was only minutes later when the same gentleman from two nights earlier took the seat next to hers. He smiled and whispered hello.

This time, Autumn looked directly into his eyes. They were dark and warm. His face was smooth and dark and he had sexy lips and high-set cheekbones. His mustache was black and neatly shaped. "Good morning," she whispered back. Heat burned her cheeks; she felt a hint of nervousness. It was not sexual, just a stir to remind her that he was so near. She looked straight ahead but saw him watch her from the corner of her eye. She smiled and tried to forget he was there. Autumn saw Betty and Emmit seated several rows ahead of her.

At first, Philip hadn't thought that she was coming to church this morning. He had waited and hoped that she would, so he could sit next to her. His brother was active in the church and had convinced Philip to go to the concert that past Friday night. Philip had agreed, and when Autumn sat next to him, he knew that he would come again and again until he got her phone number, and a chance to get to know her. He also noticed that she wasn't wearing a ring on her finger. His brother, Michael, had said she was engaged, but Autumn's mother had mentioned that the engagement was broken. He wondered why, though he wasn't sorry. All he really knew about her was that she taught school.

It was hard to concentrate on what the pastor was saying when Autumn sat so close to him. Without her looking, he got another quick glance at her. Her makeup and hair were flawless, she was dressed impeccably, and the scent of her perfume was soft, just enough to make him want to get closer to her and bury his face against her neck.

Philip was divorced, and thirty-eight. He wanted a child, and his wife had agreed, but only to make it seem as if they had enough in common to be married.

One morning while Philip was looking in her drawer, he'd found birth control pills. He'd confronted her, but he had realized before the incident that their marriage was all a lie. The birth control pills only confirmed what he already knew. He wouldn't have given up on his marriage and moved out if she hadn't pretended that she was trying to get pregnant. Although he wanted at least three children, he would have settled for one. But he couldn't tolerate the mistrust he felt for her. That was three years ago, and he still wanted to get married and start a family. His brother had the perfect life, two children, and a lovely wife. They had met in the church.

Philip was a corporate attorney for a large aerospace company in Redondo Beach, California. He was tall, muscular, and well built, with dark brown sugar–colored skin. He was a man who knew what he wanted, and once he'd made up his mind, he was relentless about getting it.

The ushers were passing the basket for the collection when Philip saw Autumn pull a five-dollar bill from her wallet. She looked up into his eyes. For an instant their eyes locked, and she smiled. A smile on a beautiful face that tugged his heart.

As she lowered her eyes, she felt an excitement that she thought had died. But, again, the excitement she felt wasn't sexual. It was calm, like a cool sea breeze that prickled against her skin. She glanced at him again as one corner of his full mouth tugged into a slight smile.

The service was over, and Autumn wondered if he would say good-bye to her. Would she see him again? Today was only the second time she had seen him at church. But seeing him at church was enough for her. She wasn't ready to date.

Everyone stood to sing the last song together and held the hand of the person next to him or her.

Her hand was slender and soft enough to be caressed. Philip could envision placing Autumn's hand against his lips. As the song ended, he was still holding her hand; he turned to face her and looked into her dark brown eyes. "I guess we will have to wait until everyone moves a little faster," Philip said. Everyone seemed to be moving slowly, and they were unable to exit the row they were in.

"Good morning, Philip. I see you've met my daughter," Betty said. She had met him a month ago. His brother had been a member of the church for ten years, but Philip didn't come very often. Mable knew the St. John family and said they were good men. Betty couldn't wait to get home to call Mable for information on Philip. Mable was a member of the church and knew everything about everyone's business, in the church.

"No, I haven't had the pleasure of meeting your daughter," he said, looking more at Autumn than he did at Betty or Emmit.

Autumn extended her hand. "I'm Autumn."

"Philip St. John."

His eyes looked into hers so deeply that Autumn could hardly look away from him until Emmit kissed her cheek. "Are you okay, daughter?"

"Yes, of course I am, Dad. I'm all right."

Philip cleared his throat. "I haven had breakfast yet. Would you care to join me, Autumn?"

"We haven't eaten yet either," Betty interjected. "Maybe we . . ."

"We're going home, Betty," Emmit interrupted. "Let them go and have a nice day."

"Okay, I'd love to go to breakfast with you, Philip. Besides, I'm hungry, too." What could she say, after all? Betty and Emmit had answered for her. Autumn smiled at her father with approval, glad he'd stopped Betty before she got started sticking her nose where it didn't belong.

"Come on, Betty. Good to see you again, Philip." He took Betty gently by her arm and led her out of the church.

Autumn watched as her parents disappeared out the door.

"There's a small restaurant in Hollywood on Melrose Boulevard. I'll drive and then bring you back to your car."

"That's okay with me," Autumn answered. People were still standing around talking, and to move out of the crowd, she had to walk in front of him.

Philip looked at her straight back and loved the way her slender hips moved as she sauntered out the door. Once they were outside and walking to the parking lot, Philip saw his brother and waved at him and his family.

"It's a nice day to take a pretty woman to breakfast."

"Thanks, and it is indeed a beautiful day. I don't think that I've seen you here on a Sunday." They were walking side by side.

"I don't go to church as much as I should. But my brother and his family go every Sunday. What about you, Autumn?"

"I don't go every Sunday, either. But I'm here at least twice a month. And I teach Sunday school sometimes."

They stopped at his black BMW, and he held the door open for Autumn.

"What do you do when you're not teaching?"

The question was complex, since she had lived a very different life. It lit a fuse to a nice, quiet day, and pulled her mind back to reality. "I go to a movie, read, and I'm a member of the PTA. There's always something to do. What do you do?"

Philip sighed. "I have a brother who lives in Hayward, California. Sometimes I drive there. I

date, but I haven't found anyone I'm serious about.
Sometimes I like to read a good mystery book when
I'm not working ten hours a day, and some Saturdays.
All in all, my life hasn't been too interesting lately.
I'm also a divorced man."

"How long have you been divorced?"

"Three years."

"Do you miss her very much?"

"No, not at all. But there are times I do miss being
married. Marriage is good as long as it's with the right
person. Do you believe that, too?" He looked over at
Autumn as the wind blew her hair against her face.

"I've never been married, but yes, I do believe it."
She was certain that Matthew would have been the
man she was going to marry, and tried to swallow
down an overwhelming sadness.

"The restaurant is around the corner."

"I take it you eat there often?"

"Not too often. But I think it's a nice place. I like
your company, Autumn, and I love your name." He
smiled when he saw her face light up, and he wondered if she had been thinking of the man she was
going to marry. Was she still hurting and in love with
him? he wondered. Philip parked the car and opened
the door for Autumn. He watched her as she climbed
out, so much a lady. He held her arm as they crossed
the busy street.

Once inside, the waitress led them to a table and
took their order. The restaurant was busy, but all
Philip could see was Autumn. The blue dress that hit
above her knees, and her wind-blown black hair. She
had an easy smile that pulled up the corners of her
delicate mouth.

"I like this place already. It's so warm and cozy,"

Autumn complimented and laid her cloth napkin across her lap.

"That's why I come here, not to mention the fact that my cousin and her husband are the owners." Philip saw his cousin and waved.

"Is that her?"

"Yes. She'll be all over the place."

Autumn watched him closely when he wasn't looking at her. He wore his clothes nicely and they were expensive, especially the gray silk shirt that he was wearing.

"Good morning," Sharon said as she looked at Autumn. She wiped her hand on her white apron.

"Good morning, and you have a crowd as usual. This is Autumn; we just left church," Philip said with pride.

"Pleased to meet you, Autumn. Why don't I get some hot coffee over here?"

"Thanks."

"You know I drink the real stuff. Make it strong," Philip said.

"I know what you like." Sharon answered and walked away with a smile on her face. *Maybe this is the woman who'll win his heart. God knows the man needs it,* she thought. She grabbed the coffee pot and started back to Philip's table. He and Autumn seemed to be in a deep conversation.

As it turned out, though, Philip and Autumn were not in deep conversation. Both of them tried to steer clear of asking personal questions or saying too much about their pasts.

After breakfast, they walked leisurely back to the car. "I'm stuffed. I haven't eaten so much in weeks," Autumn said.

"You're not dieting are you?"

"Heck no. I just don't eat breakfast often, and I missed dinner last night." She knew that she had gotten thinner, but after she'd come home from the hospital she had lost her appetite and was just gaining it back.

The ride back to where her car was parked in the church parking lot was quiet; each was thinking of the other. Philip parked his car next to Autumn's and turned around to face her. "You made my day, Autumn. I hope this is the beginning of a beautiful friendship."

"I hope so, too." She felt anxious but still, she wasn't sexually aroused by his presence or his good looks.

Philip took her hand and held it. He didn't want her to leave. She was a woman with whom, in a short time, he would fall deeply in love. "This isn't good-bye, and I would like your phone number. Maybe we can talk some time, go to a movie or just hang out together."

She smiled, and dug inside her purse for a pen and paper. She wrote down her number and handed Philip the paper.

Philip pulled out his business card and gave it to her. "You can call me anytime, either at my home or at my office. Next time, think of something that you would like to do, and we will do it." He tried to prolong the conversation to keep her just a few minutes longer.

Autumn moved closer and kissed him on the cheek. "Thanks for the breakfast. I really enjoyed it." She looked at him one last time as he got out of the car to open her door.

Autumn stepped out of the car and froze when she heard a voice.

"Mary Kay?"

For a moment she thought her heart had stopped beating. As she started to turn around, she realized that answering to the name "Mary Kay" would seem suspicious, since it wasn't really her name. As she thought of it, she doubted if she would have remembered the man's face anyway. She didn't want to and refused to look at him. So she ignored the man calling to her as Mary Kay. Her legs felt weak, and she realized that her past would haunt her to her grave. Every time she tried to forget, it was always there like a gray cloud hanging over her head to remind her of the life she'd left behind. Autumn gave Philip a half smile and got inside her car, locking the door.

Philip watched Autumn until she drove off.

Chapter 12

"Does he have any babies strolling around that you don't know about?" Lacy asked bitterly, her attempt at sarcasm not floating so blissfully by Autumn.

"No, he doesn't," Autumn snapped back, so fast that Betty closed the magazine she was reading and looked up.

"How do you know, Autumn? He could be lying. If I'd asked Eric before that little tramp came to my door, he would have said he had no children except Jordan. So how do you really know that he's not lying to you?" Lacy stood in the middle of the living room, then she took a seat on the sofa.

"He doesn't have kids," Betty answered. "That was the first question I asked Mable. She knows his family well." Betty looked as though she was proud of what she'd done and smiled.

They were at Lacy's house and Emmit had stayed at home. Lacy and Autumn looked at each other in disbelief.

"Mom, please tell me you're joking?" Autumn asked.

"No, I'm not joking. And just so you know, I ran into his brother and got some information from him, too. We were in Macy's and I recognized him."

"Eric said that you called his job and cursed him out. But he deserved it. Otherwise, I would have been totally pissed off at you," Lacy said and rolled her eyes at Betty.

"Philip called me three nights in a row. But thanks to you for nosing around in his business, I haven't heard from him since. Thanks a lot, Mom. Why would you do such a stupid thing? You give me no credit for thinking for myself. Why can't you mind your own business for a change?" Autumn hissed and turned her back to Betty.

Betty hopped off the sofa. "You listen to me, Autumn."

"No, Mom. You have gone too far this time, and I've kept my mouth shut long enough. But this time you have to know what you've done to me."

Betty looked at Lacy for help.

"Don't look at me. Autumn has a right to be pissed off. What if she really liked the man?"

Autumn grabbed her purse and started to the door, then stopped and turned around to face Betty. "I'm telling you for the last time. Let me live my own life. The next man I meet, you won't know him. You've run Philip away." She pranced out the door and slammed it behind her.

Lacy ran to the door and stuck her head out. "Don't slam my door because you are angry at Mom. You could have broken my window."

Autumn heard Lacy but didn't look back at her.

"Damn, Damn," Autumn said after she'd gotten inside the car. She and Philip had had so many good conversations and were beginning to know each other. It wasn't that she wanted to date, but they were actually becoming friends. And she needed a friend. The only thing she hadn't told him about was her sex addiction. Maybe now she wouldn't have to tell him. He would remember her for what he saw, and what she had told him.

She drove home and threw her purse on the sofa. The phone rang and she picked up.

"What now, Mom?"

"Are we having a bad day?" Philip asked.

Autumn smiled and sat down slowly on the sofa. She heard his voice, deep and vibrant.

"Betty you've been home for a whole hour and haven't said anything. So, what's wrong?" Emmit asked. After being married to her for so long, Emmit knew when she had a problem and didn't want to talk about it. But since she had been with their daughters and had come home quietly, he wanted to know what was hassling her.

Emmit had been sitting on the sofa reading the *LA Times* when Betty sat down next to him. "You know that everything I do is for the good of this family?"

"No, Betty. Everything you do is not always for the good of this family." He set the newspaper aside. "What did you do this time?"

Betty sighed. "I have never seen Autumn so angry with me. I called Philip's brother to make sure Philip wasn't another Eric. She's got enough problems of her own."

"Woman, what in the hell are you talking about?"

"All this time we thought Eric was the perfect

husband, and look how he hurt poor Lacy. Sneaking around with other women like a damn fool. If that woman wasn't stupid enough to get pregnant, we still would think he was a good man. Anyway, I told Autumn that I called Philip's brother to find out what he was like and she's really angry with me, Emmit. He hasn't called her since and they were talking every day." She looked at Emmit's accusing eyes as he stared at her. Her good deeds weren't appreciated in her family.

"Let me get a better understanding so I can look at the big picture. You went the length to get Philip's brother's phone number and asked him if Philip had any children? I guess you didn't think that Autumn had sense enough to find out about him before she got involved," Emmit said in a ferociously calm voice.

"Yes. She has a lot on her mind. I was just protecting her. But Autumn got all bent out of shape when I told her."

As she looked at Emmit, his face was filled with accusation, and for a stunned instant she thought she saw a glimmer of revulsion that stabbed at her heart and frightened her.

"Betty, don't you think that Autumn has enough sense to ask him that? Do you really think she's that stupid or gullible to think that he may not have ever been married or had children? Even if she didn't ask, it wasn't your business to." Emmit got up and went to the den. He could no longer look at her, and it was getting harder and harder to live with Betty. Being married to her was exhausting.

Betty got up and went into the den behind Emmit. "Are you so angry that you can't sit next to me?"

"Listen, Betty. You go to the beauty salon and gossip to the operators about what your clients tell you in confidence the day before. Then you come home and call someone else to tell them. You're in everyone's business except your own. When was the last time we had sex?"

"What?" She looked at him as though he had gone crazy. "We had sex two nights ago."

"That's all it was, too. There was no passion, or no interest from you. You have time for everyone else but me. Last Sunday when Philip asked Autumn to go to breakfast, you wanted to intrude. Now why would he want her parents to go? Mrs. Fields doesn't speak to you because you told her about her husband and the woman who goes to your beauty salon. You're in everyone's business. Now Autumn has probably lost a good man. She's still hurting over Matthew. Now, thanks to you, she has lost Philip, too. But I forgot, you were only trying to help her." Emmit got up and got his hat and jacket.

"Where are you going?"

"I don't know, Betty. I can't live with you much longer. It's not working out for me. But right now I need some fresh air. The air in this house has gone stale."

His tone was irascible, his words perverse. Betty looked at Emmit with her mouth hanging open. She got up and walked around the house, stopping to look at their family pictures during their happier years. Her girls were ten and twelve, and Emmit was home on leave. But even then she was the head of the household. Being in the service, he was always in a different state, and Betty had to raise the girls her way. Now Emmit had the nerve to disagree with every decision she made as though she had to get his permission. Well, she was not the kind of wife that needed a man to tell her what to do. One would think that after so many years Emmit would know her.

Betty had come from a long line of strong women in her family. Her father was in a car accident. After the accident, most of the time he was unable to work. He was a soft-spoken man. Her mother worked hard and paid most of the bills while he stayed home and drowned his sorrows in a wine bottle. After working hard for so many years and taking care of his family, it was hard for him to be disrespected by his wife for not being the strong man that he once was. Finally, her mother threw him out, and he'd moved in with his mother. When he died, his family had turned their backs on his wife and children. But the more Betty tried not to be like her mother, the more she discovered that she was. Except Emmit had a job, and she prayed that he didn't leave her. She had tried to change her independent habits, though it was hard and she wasn't being herself when she did things his way. So he kept quiet until he was filled with the anger he displayed today.

Now Emmit was gone and Betty had no idea where he was or when he would be back.

"We need to make plans, Lacy. I want to come home to you and Jordan." Eric stood in the living room and Lacy was sitting in a chair facing him. "Where is Jordan?" Eric asked.

"He's across the street with Jamie. Listen, Eric, I told you until she has the baby, we haven't anything to discuss."

"She had the baby yesterday."

Lacy felt her chest tighten and her heart quicken with dread. "I thought she had two months."

"She did, but she went into labor yesterday and lost the baby. She was born dead."

"Too bad. Now you think that you can come back and we can pick up our lives where we left off?"

"We agreed that if the baby wasn't mine we would get back together. It's not all my fault you know."

Lacy's head jerked up fast and she stared at him. "What do you mean it's not your fault? I wasn't the one who cheated."

"No, not with another man. But you didn't appreciate anything I did for you. When was the last time you said that you loved me, the last time you initiated the lovemaking between us, or the last time you said thank you about anything?" He sighed and sat next to her. "I know that I hurt you terribly, but you have to take some of the blame. I needed to feel wanted for more than help paying bills."

Lacy turned around to face him. "You're not going to place the blame on me for your cheating. I could have married any man I wanted, but no, I married you. After you cheated I didn't run into another man's arms. Instead of skirting around with another woman, you could have talked to me." She placed her hands over her eyes and cried.

Eric pulled her into his arms. To his surprise she didn't resist. Instead, she closed her eyes and held him. "I want to go and get Jordan, and I want to stay tonight and bring my clothes back tomorrow."

Lacy released herself from him and sat up straight. "It's your house, too. But don't expect too much too soon. And if you haven't cut all ties with that girl, then don't come back. I don't want to confuse my son."

"Do you really think I've been trying to come home and make you forgive me if I was going to see her again? We never had an affair, Lacy, it was just sex."

"Like I said, don't expect too much too soon. It's going to take time to get this marriage the way it was."

"Well, I hope both of us try. It takes two to make a good marriage."

The nerve of him, she thought. *I didn't cheat, and I won't change for him.* Any man in his right mind would want me, she thought. *I brought class into Eric's life. He had nothing until he married me, and he knows it.*

Eric waited for Lacy to answer; with disappointment she only stared at him and rolled her eyes up toward the ceiling.

"I'll go and get Jordan," Eric said.

Lacy went to the window and watched Eric go into the neighbor's house across the street. It was already October and cool. It looked as though Los Angeles would get rain early that year. She saw Eric and Jordan coming out of the house. Lacy looked at her son bouncing beside his dad; he looked happy and was chatting cheerfully. He had asked questions that Lacy and Eric couldn't answer to make him understand. Lacy often wondered how she would explain to Jordan that his father had a baby by another woman. She smiled to herself. Now she wouldn't have to worry about it anymore.

Chapter 13

Autumn was anticipating the PTA meetings again and beginning to feel that her life was getting back to normal. She and Philip had been talking all week. It was Saturday morning, and the school festival started at 9:00 AM. There would be booths lined up around the playground. One was for selling popcorn, one for hot dogs and sodas, and another one for cakes and pies. There were rides for the children and books to purchase, and Philip would be there around 11:00 AM. What a wonderful man he was.

Matthew never joined her for any of the school activities that she participated in. She had her career and he had his, but he always acted as if his career was more valuable.

Autumn was fond of Philip, but the thought of telling him about her sex addiction frightened her. Although he was a handsome man, she still felt no sexual urges for him, and she didn't want to hurt him or lose their friendship. She couldn't bear to look at the disappointment in his eyes when she told him the truth, and it had to be soon. He would lose all respect for her; she wasn't ready to stop seeing him, and sooner or later he would want to make love.

When Philip arrived, Autumn was standing at the popcorn stand talking to one of the students that was helping. She saw him stop and purchase a grape soda. He was dressed casually in his jeans, looking tall and breathtakingly handsome. Her heart beat erratically as he slowly walked toward her.

"I see you're wearing jeans today, too," Autumn said.

"Yeah, but you look better in yours." He touched her hair and kissed her left cheek. She led him around the playground.

"Would you like to see my classroom?"

"Sure. Lead the way."

"Come on. It's Room 22." Autumn unlocked the door and held it open as he stepped inside.

"It's nice. If I had a child I would want you to be her teacher."

"Her?"

"Well, girl or boy. I would want you to be the teacher." He looked around at the pictures on the wall of her past and present students.

"Why would you want me to be your child's teacher?" she asked, following him.

"Because it's easy to tell that you care about your students. One could tell by the way the classroom is decorated." He placed one arm around her waist as she stood next to him.

Feeling his hand on her, she felt sexy and so close to him. For the first time, she wanted to kiss him and wondered what it would feel like if they made love, not just sex for a quick fix until the next time she needed it, but really make love, feeling the passion in every fiber of her body. After she told him the truth about her past life, would he ever want to see her again? He treated her gently, like a precious flower. She wouldn't be the decent woman and fifth-grade teacher that he saw now. Maybe he was too good for her, and to think that he wanted the schoolteacher and precious flower made her heart ache. Lord, she thought. What woman could resist him?

After Autumn and Philip walked around the grounds, she was proud to introduce him to her peers. At 1:00 PM, they left.

"What do you have planned for the rest of today?" Philip asked.

"I hadn't made any plans. But I do need to go to my apartment to make a couple of phone calls. Why don't we have lunch?"

"I was hoping that you would ask. Do we need to stop and buy anything?" He couldn't stop himself and gave her another quick kiss on her cheek.

Autumn smiled and grabbed his hand to lead him to their cars. "How about pizza?"

"And beer?" he asked.

"And beer," she replied and laughed. That was another thing she loved about him. He made her laugh so easily. "There is a Shaky's Pizza on the way."

Philip walked Autumn to her car. She was wearing a red sweater that emphasized her perfectly sized breasts. The jeans were tight across her hips, and she had a sexy walk that made him want to watch her all day. He shook his head to calm the excitement in his mind, but what man didn't want to be in love with a woman that aroused him every time he thought of her?

"I won't drive too fast, so don't get lost." She

started her car and waited until Philip had gotten inside of his.

Autumn pulled out of the lot first, and Philip followed. She peeked in her rearview mirror to make sure he was following her. She drove slowly enough to prevent losing him. This would be his first time at her apartment, and she was jittery. Would he want to sleep with her? Oh no, she thought.

Shaky's Pizza was only a twenty-minute drive from the school. She pulled up in the parking lot and Philip parked beside her.

"While you are ordering the pizza, I'll run across the street and buy the beer." He pulled out a twenty-dollar bill and pushed it into her hand.

"Oh, no, Philip. I invited you to lunch."

"Take the money, woman. Next time you pay." Before Autumn could oppose any further, he had stepped away.

She went inside Shaky's Pizza and placed her order. The place was boisterous, with small children playing on the video game machines and running around tables. As she waited, she thought of Philip and smiled inwardly. She was beginning to feel calm. He was a gentleman, after all. All the reasons to make her fall in love with him. Yet it was all the reasons for her not to. She didn't want to hurt him and still had to tell him about her shady past. But not today; today she just wanted to laugh and be happy.

She was pulled out of a daze when her number was called. She picked up the pizza and went outside. Philip was waiting inside his car. She waved, and he followed her to her apartment.

Autumn unlocked the door and they went inside. "You have a seat, and I'll get some plates and glasses.

On her way to the kitchen, she turned on the radio. "Sorry I don't have any new CDs. When I'm home I'm either correcting school papers or watching TV."

"Don't worry about it. The radio is good enough. Besides, I'll help you and have a seat when we are ready to eat," Philip answered and placed the beer on the table.

Once in the small kitchen, Autumn got two plates from the cabinet and gave Philip two tall glasses.

They went to the dining area, and Autumn sat at the table. Philip sat opposite her.

"You have a nice place, Autumn. Did you decorate it yourself?" he asked, and looked around at the exquisite paintings on the wall.

"I sure did. I love decorating." Autumn took a bite from her pizza. "Did you decorate your home?"

"Yes, and it looks like a 'man' home. It needs a woman's touch. Looking at your colors, I realize now that I have too many browns and blacks. Your apartment is bright and cheery. This place is you." He filled the glasses with beer and noticed that everything was neatly in place.

"Are you going to church tomorrow morning?" Autumn asked.

"No. I have a report that is due on Monday morning." He didn't want to tell her that he usually did the Monday report on Saturday mornings but today he'd wanted to be with her. "Are you going?"

Autumn smiled and shook her head. "No. I have papers to correct that I didn't do this morning." She placed her pizza back on the plate. The phone rang, and she wiped her hand. "Excuse me," Autumn said and rushed to the phone.

She was standing as she talked on the phone.

When she sat down in the chair, Philip could see that she was disappointed about something. Aggravated, she hung up and shook her head as she came back to the table.

"Is everything all right?" Philip asked.

"It's nothing serious, but I am disappointed. I signed the waiting list for the new homes in Inglewood behind Hollywood Park, but I was too late."

"My brother and his family just moved into theirs. They are nice homes, too."

"I wanted one of the Traditions. Originally, I had my name on the list for the new Liemert Park homes, but they haven't started building yet and are behind schedule. I'm beginning to wonder if they will."

"I'm sorry, baby. Living in a gated community is safe for single women." But he wasn't being completely truthful. If they got serious, she could move in with him in Walnut. His three-bedroom home was lonely. And since he'd met Autumn, the house seemed even bigger than before.

Philip was mesmerized with the sight of Autumn. She had more sex appeal than any woman he'd known, and her beauty was invigorating. Every time he looked at her, he saw a different beauty than before. And the red sweater was driving him crazy.

"Philip?"

"I'm sorry. I was thinking of the report I have to do," he lied and wondered what she would think of him if he told her the truth. "What are you doing when you finish correcting papers tomorrow?"

"I haven't thought about it yet." she answered.

Philip took another drink of his beer. "Nice and cold; this is the way I like my beer." He placed the glass on the table, reached over, and touched Autumn's hand. "Why don't we do something together?"

Autumn felt a stir that she thought had disappeared. What was on his mind? He looked so sexy in his T-shirt and jeans. "Okay, what?"

"We have time to think about it. No hurry. I love spending time with you, Autumn." Their eyes locked as he rubbed her hand. "How many children do you want?"

Her pizza caught in her throat and she began coughing. His question had completely astonished her. Her eyes started to water and she wiped them with the napkin in front of her.

"Sweetheart, are you all right?" Philip asked with concern.

"Yes, and I'm so embarrassed." She cleared her throat.

"Don't be. Here, take a drink of the beer."

"I used to want four children. Two boys and two girls, but now I'll settle for one. Why do you ask?" She wondered what was he thinking as she gave him a inquisitive glance.

"I just wondered and wanted to know if we were on the same page. I would love to have a child." He was enthralled with her good looks. Her smooth skin glowed. Sweet and soft and warm was what he thought of her. It was hard to draw his eyes from her, or stop thinking of kissing her full, sexy mouth. She looked as though she knew what he was thinking. But how could she, how could she know how much he really wanted her?

"Do you like jazz?" Autumn asked.

"Yes. Actually, I like all music, but I love jazz."

"There's a club in Redondo Beach that has a very

good jazz band. I thought maybe we could go, have a glass of wine, and enjoy the music." She placed her glass back on the table, and for a second, Philip, thought he saw a flicker of indecision in her eyes.

"Sounds great."

Autumn looked at the hair that peeked from his V-neck T-shirt and felt a tremor; her stomach clenched. And again, she felt a tremor of excitement at wanting him, needing him to hold her in his strong arms and never let her go. Autumn was sure that the tremors she felt weren't for sex, but for someone for whom she really cared. She knew that she couldn't have him until she told him about her past. Inside her heart, she knew he would leave her like Matthew did. She had to tell him soon; she couldn't bear another excruciating heartache.

They both had two slices of pizza and talked until eight-thirty. Autumn had found herself laughing more than she had in months. For the moment, her life felt normal again.

Philip glanced at his watch. "Well, I better go now, but I'm looking forward to tomorrow."

Autumn walked him to the door; before she realized it, she was in his arms. He kissed her until she felt dizzy. *What a good kisser he is,* she thought, barely opening her eyes when he let her go.

Philip's heart had drowned in her kiss. He wanted to make love to her, make her ask for more. But he knew it hadn't been too long since her breakup with Matthew. He wanted her past behind her, so she would want no one but him. Then he would make her love him, and only him. With dread, he let her go.

* * *

The next morning Autumn slept late, got up, and corrected her school papers. Every time she thought of her date with Philip, she felt nervous. Was she really ready for this? She thought of Matthew, and the pain didn't seem to stab her heart like before.

The evening was approaching, and Autumn was even more apprehensive about her date with Philip, but the more she saw him the more she wanted to know about him. She loved watching his every move. He reminded her of a young boy when he smiled. Despite fighting with herself, she wanted to become closer to him. She was beginning to feel she had no control over the way she felt about him, and it was frightening. She knew that she was playing with fire.

Dressed in a black dress that stopped above her knees, she was ready when the doorbell rang. Autumn ambled to the living room and opened the door. He was standing there, tall and good-looking, with a wide smile that made her feel chills up and down her spine.

"You look beautiful, as usual," Philip complimented. He stepped inside and brushed past her.

"Thanks. I'll get my purse and we can be on our way." When she got to her bedroom, Autumn took a quick glance in the mirror one last time. She ran her fingers through her hair and sighed. "I wonder how the night will end," she thought out loud, and strutted out of the bedroom.

The band was already playing on stage when Autumn and Philip entered the club. They were led to a small table in the middle of the room, with Philip behind her looking at a pair of absolutely sensational legs. He sat next to her and ordered wine.

Autumn was conscious of him being so close. He held her hand and gave her a quick kiss on her cheek.

As the night wore on she welcomed his close presence, the scent of his cologne, and the way he looked at her as though he adored her. Philip was a man who was hard to resist. He made her feel alive again, and she felt a passionate intensity between them and knew that he felt it, too. It was thick enough to cut with a knife. "Do you like the music?" Philip whispered close to her ear.

"I love it. I'm happy that we came here."

An hour passed and Autumn knew that she had to do something. She wanted Philip but couldn't have him. If they made love, and she told him later, it was more than a probability that he would hate her as much as Matthew did. As she thought about it, she thought why tell him at all when she could just stop seeing him? At least she would go out with respect. Not seeing Philip again made her feel ill inside. She had to swallow hard to clear the dryness in her throat. Despite the dull pain in her heart, and with all fairness to Philip, tonight would be their last night together.

Taking a deep breath, Autumn leaned against him. "I don't feel well. I'm so sorry, Philip, but I need to go home."

"Of course, I will take you home. We could have stayed at your apartment and I could have taken care of you." He took her hand to lead her from the table.

Once inside the car, Philip held her hand. "Maybe you are coming down with the flu. It's going around, you know." He kissed her on the cheek and started up the car.

"I'm sure it is the flu. I'm so sorry that we had to cut our date short, but I'll go to bed, and tomorrow I'm sure that I'll feel better."

"I can stay the night if you need me to."

"No!" she all but yelled before she realized the word was out of her mouth. She looked at the frown on Philip's face. He looked confused and hurt.

"I mean no, I wouldn't want you to catch it if it's really the flu. But I do appreciate your offer."

They were silent the rest of the drive home. Philip parked the car and got out to help Autumn.

This was going to be harder than she realized, for both of them. In her heart, she didn't want to stop seeing Philip. Autumn unlocked the door and stepped inside. She wanted to stop Philip at the door but couldn't.

Philip took Autumn by her hand and led her to the sofa. They sat facing each other. "I can sleep here on the sofa. You don't have to be alone tonight, Autumn."

She wanted to cry. He was a good man, the man that every woman dreamed of spending her life with. She saw compassion in him that Matthew had lacked.

Autumn touched his hand. "Philip, I need to tell you something about my past."

"I don't want to know about your past, Autumn. We can start new and forget the past. It doesn't matter who we were before, who we are now is what's important to me."

"But, Philip. You need to listen."

"No. You need to listen. Are you still in love with the man you had planned to marry? If you are, I'll leave and never look back."

Moments passed and she couldn't answer. Autumn wanted to fall into his arms, she wanted him to hold her and never let her go, but she couldn't. She couldn't hurt him. "No, I'm not in love with him. You helped me get over the pain that I carried inside of me."

"Then, that's all I need to know about you." He stood up, and with both her hands, he pulled her up with him.

Autumn felt his arms around her waist, his warm lips against hers, and tasted the wine on her tongue. She circled her arms around his neck and sank miserably into his kiss; his tongue sought hers. She wanted to kiss him all night. When Philip let her go, she was too weak to remain standing alone, and she held his arm.

"We don't need to talk anymore tonight. You go to bed, and tomorrow I'll call you."

Autumn watched him stroll out the door and flopped down on the sofa. "You coward," she whispered. She placed both hands against her face and laid her head back against the sofa. "Why didn't you tell him?" Now she had to toss and turn all night before she told him tomorrow.

"Hi, girl," Autumn said as she walked inside of Lacy's house. "I see Mom's car, where is she?"

"In the backyard picking grapefruit off the tree. I wish she could take the tree home with her. I don't eat grapefruit, and I have no need for a grapefruit tree. She claims that she's on a diet, but she looks larger to me."

Lacy took a seat on the sofa and Autumn sat in the chair opposite her.

"She's only a little overweight, and she still looks good. I'm still not my usual size," Autumn said.

"I know. You are still too thin if you ask me. Are you eating?"

"Sure I'm eating, and I have a lot on my mind. I'm

still trying to get my life back together. I was out there for almost a year, but it seems that I'll be punished for the rest of my life for my mistakes."

Lacy rolled her eyes. "Don't be so dramatic, Autumn. Everyone has some kind of secret in their lives. And no, Matthew won't be in your life. Get over it. Maybe it wasn't meant for you to marry him. Believe me, honey, he's not losing any sleep over it."

"I know, and I'm over him, even though I still wonder what could have been. But I don't blame him for leaving me. Any man would have." She thought of Philip and felt her eyes burn.

"I wouldn't say any man," Betty said as she entered the living room. "Matthew wants the perfect wife, and perfect world. He won't find it with any woman. How are you and Philip getting along? Now, that's a real man. He reminds me of your father when he was young."

"It's time I tell Philip about my past so that I can get on with my life and he can get on with his."

Lacy looked at Autumn in disbelief. "Tell him the truth about what? I know you're not planning on telling Philip about that terrible illness. Why in hell does he need to know anyway? Mom, you need to talk some sense into her."

"Autumn, are you trying to run the man away, because he doesn't need to know. Honey, he's not going to tell you everything about himself." Betty took a seat beside Autumn. "Let the man love and respect you for who you really are. That wasn't really you, baby. Telling Philip would only be introducing him to a different person."

"But, Mom, he wants to get serious. He hasn't said

it yet, but I know he does. I lost Matthew by not telling him."

"No, you lost Matthew because you slept with someone who knew him. You're not sleeping around anymore, Autumn. There is no reason to destroy a perfectly good relationship with a man who cares about you. Now have you been getting any sexual urges for him?"

Lacy's ears perked up, and she waited for Autumn's answer.

When Autumn saw Betty and Lacy exchange glances, her eyes dropped. "Yes, but differently than before."

"Good. You are a normal woman with normal cravings. Don't tell him, Autumn. He doesn't want to know. I told your father that he was the first man that I slept with, and that's what he wanted to know. Hundreds of women have told their husbands the same thing."

"What if Philip and I are together and a man recognizes me?"

"You tell him that he is mistaken. Didn't you say that you never used your real name?" Lacy asked. "Besides, it's too late to worry about it now. Lots of women were prostitutes before they were married, and their husbands never knew it"

"Well thank you for comparing me with a prostitute. I never realized that I was so close to becoming one," Autumn snapped.

"I didn't mean it that way, and don't get angry at me because your bed is cold at night."

"She was just trying to talk some sense into you, Autumn. You developed an illness that you didn't ask for. Don't tell him, honey."

Autumn nodded in agreement. "I want to talk about something else. I had forgotten to tell you that I didn't get one of the new houses in Inglewood. I was too far down on the list."

"I don't know why you are so disappointed. There are homes here in Westchester that you can purchase, and the price is no higher. I can't understand why you would buy in Inglewood anyway. You can even wait until the houses are built in Liemert Park. The neighborhood is well established and near Baldwin Hills," Lacy said.

Autumn looked at Lacy for a few moments before she spoke. "Are you and Eric getting along?"

Betty looked incredulously at Autumn but didn't say anything. She could see the anger written on Autumn's face, and wondered why Lacy had missed it.

"We get up every morning and go to our jobs, come home, and Eric spends most of his evenings with Jordan," she said, waving a well-manicured hand. "He has a bug up his ass because I won't let him jump all over me in bed." Lacy shifted position on the sofa and blew her hair from her forehead.

"Well, it seems that my bed isn't the only cold one at night. Your husband sleeps with you in a cold bed. Tell me, Lacy. Does a lock of your hair stray out of place while you are having sex, or do you hold on to it? Are you always so fake and impersonal? Does anyone's feelings even matter to you, except your own?" Autumn watched Lacy's face as her brows knitted together, her mouth hung open.

"Just because I like the best in life doesn't mean I'm fake."

Autumn stood up and held her purse in her hand. "But you are fake, inconsiderate, and conceited."

Lacy stood up quickly. "Look, Autumn, just because you're having trouble with Philip, don't take your anger out on me."

"All right, girls. That's quite enough," Betty interrupted. She had heard enough.

Without looking back, Autumn strutted out the door and slammed it behind her.

"She gets angry too easily. You really need to talk to her, Mom. The nerve, coming into my house crying for advice and then getting nasty with me for no reason at all, and insulting me, I might add," Lacy hissed. She crossed her arms across her chest and threw her head up in a haughty gesture.

"She needed advice, Lacy." Betty waved her hand dismissively. "What's the use?" She grabbed her jacket and started to the door.

Walking across the street to her car, Autumn felt a cool, balmy breeze against her face. She needed to feel the fresh air. Today wasn't a day that she could tolerate Lacy's insults. She doubted if Lacy was even aware of how arrogant she really was.

When Betty got outside, Autumn had already driven off. She released a deep sigh. Emmit had said that he needed to talk to her, and she dreaded the drive home.

Autumn got home and checked her messages. The first one was from Philip. He wanted to know if she was feeling better today. Last night he'd brought her home early because she pretended that she was ill, and then he called her in the morning and she was not home. As Autumn listened to his message, she wondered what he'd thought when he didn't reach her. Thinking of what Betty and Lacy said, she flopped down on the sofa. Don't tell Philip about your past, she kept hearing in her head. But would she always be looking over her shoulder to see if someone recognized her? No, she had to tell Philip. He would be disappointed, but he would forget her and find a woman that was worthy of him.

Autumn picked up the phone and dialed Philip's number. The phone and doorbell rang at the same time. She hung up and opened the door. It was Philip.

Autumn eyes were wide with surprise as though he'd bolted from the blue, but she managed a smile. "Come in. I was dialing your phone number and hung up to answer the door." She led him to the sofa and sat next to him.

"I was concerned when I called and you weren't home."

"I went to see my sister. Would you like a cup of coffee, juice?"

"How about coffee?"

"Sure." She left the living room and came back with a sliver tray and two cups of coffee. "I'm glad you came over. I really have something to talk to you about, Philip." She gave him his cup and sipped from hers. "You see, I need to tell you something about my past. I have made some mistakes, and I want to be honest with you."

Philip sipped the coffee and placed the cup on the coffee table. Autumn started to speak again, but he placed his finger to her lips. "Autumn, you didn't murder anyone did you, you don't have AIDS?"

"No. No, of course not."

"Then there isn't anything to tell me about your past. Do you care about me as much as I care about you?"

"Yes, I care deeply for you."

"Then, why don't we concentrate on what we have now? The past is the past, and believe me, we all have one. No one is perfect, baby." He placed his hand against her chin and held her face up, then kissed her tenderly on her lips. Every time he saw her, he wanted her lips against his. Sweet, he thought.

She was relieved and circled her arms around his neck, felt him hold her tighter. She wanted him, wanted to please him. Her mind floated lightly as the kiss deepened.

"You are so sweet, Autumn," he whispered against her ear. "I want you to belong to me." He pulled away but held her hand. "I must be honest with you. I want a committed relationship, and I don't want to play the dating game. It's too exhausting, and it's you that I want."

"I feel exactly the same." He looked deeply into her eyes, and she knew that he wanted her. Autumn stood up and extended her hand, then led him to her bedroom. They stood in the middle of the room and held each other; he gave her a long, urgent kiss that made her knees weak. They both needed the other. This would be her commitment to him.

It surprised Autumn at how much she wanted him, how much she really wanted to love him. After Matthew, and her past with men, she had never imagined that she would feel the need to be loved again. While kissing him, she felt his hands rubbing the middle of her back; he continued to stroke her, surprising her with his gentleness.

Philip pulled her down on the bed. Her eyes were closed as he looked at her peaceful, beautiful face.

Slowly her eyes opened, glowing with love. She rose slightly to his touch as his tongue stoked the tip of her exposed, brown nipple, and continued inflaming her with his warm touch. Autumn's heart was beating rapidly as she felt the excitement building up her thighs. He simply made her feel loved.

They were naked when he climbed on top and entered her, her legs wrapping around his waist.

Autumn felt the difference of being made love to rather than just having the passion for sex. It was all so real. Not the fictitious life that she had led with strange men. So many times she closed her eyes to prevent seeing the other men, to prevent herself from remembering their faces, their smells, or their sounds. With Philip, she felt the excitement, and yet she felt peaceful. Was she falling in love with him?

Philip pushed deeper inside her, and she moaned, lost in multiple orgasms that rocked her soul.

He lay beside her, holding her in his arms. "How do you feel?"

Autumn faced him and held herself up on her arm. "I feel good, and you?"

"Like I've found the woman that I've been searching for all my life. You're the only woman I want. We are good together and I love being with you. Does that sum it up?"

"Yes, and I agree. I'm the only woman I want you to be with. I'm glad that you came over." She closed her eyes and moved closer to him.

"Do you feel better than you did last night?"

For an instant he seemed familiar to Autumn, like she'd known him before. But she knew that it was only because she felt as though she had known him longer, felt so relaxed with him. "I feel much, much better than I did last night."

He ran his long fingers through her hair and rose up to kiss her shoulder. He wanted to keep touching and loving her and pulled Autumn on top of him. He entered her again; her face glowed and her eyes were closed. Philip had never seen such a beautiful picture.

Chapter 14

Emmit looked at the large wooden clock on the wall. He had been home for an hour. Betty was home when he'd arrived and had been on the phone without acknowledging his presence. When he'd arrived, he'd given her a quick kiss on the cheek, but she'd waved and kept on talking. Was he so boring that she would rather talk about the business of her clients than to spend time with her husband? Emmit wondered. She had taken her marriage for granted and for too long. Yesterday she was home before him and had gone shopping when he got home.

Life was so good with June. She was a sexy woman and a sensational lover. June was conscientious and loved having him with her. Emmit shook his head in disgust as he thought of how much he really missed her; Betty was a constant reminder of the love he lost.

"Emmit, are you ready for dinner?" Betty asked while blocking the television.

"I ate my dinner an hour ago, Betty. You were on the phone. Would you please step aside so I can see the TV?" he snapped without looking at her.

She moved. "When did you eat?"

He sighed as though he was being disturbed. But he was angry, tired, and wondered what to do about their marriage. "Come here, Betty, and sit next to me. I told you yesterday that we needed to talk, but you seem to have forgotten." He stared at her as she hesitated, finally sitting down on the sofa next to him.

Betty dreaded every minute of it. She knew that Emmit wasn't happy, but she honestly didn't know what to do about it. He used to be so easy to get along with, never asked for anything, and he never demanded much from her.

"We're living in the same house, Betty, but I don't feel as though I have a wife. This empty life may be enough for you, but it isn't a marriage."

"I know you're not happy, but it's been this way between us for so long that I don't know what to do to change it."

"You'll never know, and I don't think you want to. It's not entirely all your fault. I let this void in our marriage go too long before I got tired and could no longer tolerate it."

The feeling of disturbance deep inside her was overwhelmingly frightful because she still loved her husband. The last time Emmit put a distance between them, it was so painful that she thought she would wither away like a flower left too long without rain. She needed Emmit too much to lose him.

"Emmit, please don't leave me again," she murmured.

"I promised that I would stay and see if we could salvage our marriage. But I'm a man and not a picture on the wall. I love being married, but to the right person. We don't have a marriage. Hell, all you need is our daughters and that damn beauty shop. I need a woman who needs me, too. I need a real woman, Betty. One that I can feel and touch."

She was getting angry. "What . . . am I if not a woman?"

"You're a woman who only needs her husband to pay the bills. You make all the decisions, and you are too damn nosey. You worry about Lacy and Autumn and your clients when you have enough here to worry about. Stay out of our daughters' business; you only make life worse."

Betty jumped up off the sofa. "Who went to Autumn's meetings with her? Who was there to support her when she needed it? Well, it sure wasn't you." She rested both hands on her hips.

"I was never involved because you convinced Autumn to keep her illness a secret from me. If I had known she was going out nights and sleeping with different men, maybe I could have stopped her. Maybe she wouldn't have been beaten. Did you ever think of that? But no, you had to take control and fuck everything up," he yelled bitterly. "You have the audacity to talk to me as though I haven't been here for my girls." As he spoke, he got angrier, his eyes full of hostility. He had tried his damnedest to be a good husband and father. Betty would be the wife he had married for a few months, then go right back to her usual unresponsive, noncommittal ways as though he wasn't around. His daughters were adults with their own lives, so where did it leave him? Sure, he could go back to June, but he knew that trying to salvage his marriage was the right thing to do. Besides, he'd promised Betty that he would try. But now he was tired.

Betty saw the flash of anger in Emmit's eyes when she sat back on the sofa and he turned to face her. He had made it bluntly apparent that she was losing him.

"I'm so ready to pack my bags and get the hell out of here. There's no life, no joy or happiness for me anymore."

Betty listened while she tried to think of something to say to calm Emmit's anger. She sat close to him and held his hand.

He stared at her with exasperation written all over his face. What was she up to? But he was too angry and fed up to soften the blow of his decision to leave her.

"Emmit, before you do something crazy like divorce me, I think we should take a week off and go on a vacation. We are at the age to be enjoying our lives. I know that I haven't made it possible, but I'd like to start now."

"Look, Betty . . ."

"No," she said. "Just listen to me. I'll do whatever it takes to spend the rest of my life with you. You could have left me, but you were willing to make another try at our marriage, so you still care for me."

He was ready to divorce Betty, but once again, he had to listen to her proposal.

"Emmit, can't we go someplace that's romantic? We may not agree on everything, but we both agree on the good sex we have together." She smiled and felt the excitement stirring inside her just by speaking of the urges she still had for him. For a middle-aged couple, they still had an active sex life.

Emmit shook his head and sighed. "Where do you want to go?"

"How about a trip to Hawaii? You mentioned it last

year, but nothing ever came of it. We could go for seven days, and the airlines have a special."

He looked at her face; she looked sad, yet optimistic. "How long will it be before you go back to your old self again?" he asked grimly.

"Emmit, I know now that I have to change. Autumn is hardly speaking to me, and Lacy says I should take care of my business and stay out of theirs. They are not my girls any longer. They're my daughters, and they can take care of their own lives. It's time for us."

"Okay. Tomorrow make reservations for the trip."

Betty reached over and kissed his cheek. "Thank you, Emmit."

Betty got up and went to shower. She stood under the hot water with her eyes closed as the water dripped down her back. She was relieved as she made mental notes in her head about the trip. She would make her marriage last, and she still loved her husband and couldn't live knowing that he would meet another woman. Betty vowed that she wouldn't be alone like some of her clients who were over fifty. Most of them were alone and didn't have a man. All they talked about was how hard it was to get a good man, and how lucky she was to have one so handsome. Now all she had to do was keep him.

Autumn was happier than she had been in a long time. She no longer needed more than one man for sex; nor was she afraid that she had to tell Philip about her past. He said that her past didn't matter, but would he still mean it if he found out? The question nagged at her constantly. She had completely fallen in love with Philip, and he said that he was in love with her, too. He'd even asked her if she ever wanted to get married.

It was seven that evening and Autumn was expecting Philip. She had showered and changed into a pair of navy sweats and a sleeveless T-shirt. Not wearing shoes, Autumn padded in from the kitchen when she heard the doorbell ring.

She opened the door, and Philip grabbed her into his arms. "I couldn't wait to see you, baby." He gave her a long, blissful kiss, and she responded passionately. They sat together closely on the sofa. She laid her head on his shoulder.

"How was your day at school?"

"It was busy. I may teach summer school this year. But it's only half days."

"What do you do when you are not teaching summer school?"

"I go to the beach and read a good book, sleep later, and eat too much." She smiled and kissed him on his cheek. "Are you jealous because you have to work the summer months?"

"For the first time I am jealous. I could be sleeping late in the mornings with you." He held both sides of her face and gave her a deep, passionate kiss. She felt his hand move under her blouse, and in minutes they were in her bedroom.

They undressed each other and got in bed. He kissed every part of her body, and she purred. He went inside her slowly, so slowly that when she breathed his name, she felt a rippling sensation spreading all through her body. Her orgasms were quick and hot, and when he arched his back, a deep moan escaped from his throat. He went slowly, longer, then wildly as she cried out with pleasure. He rolled off her and their bodies dripped with sweat. She was insatiable, and he loved her.

She lay in his arms, their bodies limp. The room was quiet and peaceful just as their worlds were.

"I don't want to go home," he whispered.

"Don't go. Stay with me tonight."

He stayed and held her close in his arms. They were still in the same position when they woke up the next morning and made love again.

The weeks went by quickly and Autumn and Philip fell deeply in love. They spent their weekends together and talked on the phone every night. Autumn wondered why was she so lucky. The life she had lived was behind her and replaced with a loving, good man. God, how lucky she was.

Chapter 15

"Why are you staring at me, Lacy?"

"You look different. In the past when you came to see me you were always so sad. Either it was Matthew or that sex problem. But today I don't see the frowns and stress written all over your face. You actually look happy."

"I am happy," Autumn replied.

"Is it Philip? You two seem to be seeing a lot of each other, and it's time the family met him."

"Yes, it's Philip. He gave me my life back. I'm happier with him than I was the entire time I was with Matthew. Philip is easier to talk with, and I can be myself with him. It's almost like we've met before in another time and place." And it was true, it was as though they were old friends.

"I'm happy for you. Just don't fall too hard. The harder you fall, the more it hurts."

Autumn looked at Lacy with frustration. She could never say anything good without turning it into a pessimistic scenario. They were standing in the kitchen, and Lacy gave Autumn a glass of orange juice. As they talked, Autumn followed Lacy back into the living room.

Autumn sat in the chair and sighed. She couldn't ignore Lacy's comment.

"That's the attitude I don't like. I don't want to worry about falling too hard. I want to be in a relaxed relationship and let the chips fall where they may. Philip is different, and I love him."

"Just don't fall with the chips. I don't want to see you hurt or ill again. I'm just concerned."

Poor, Lacy. She was never happy, and when she was unhappy she wanted everyone around her to be unhappy, too. Her way of thinking was so perplexing.

"How is Eric?"

"He's okay, and we're sleeping together again."

"But . . . ?" Autumn asked. She knew there had to be more to them just sleeping together. Looking at Lacy, one could see that she was miserable.

Lacy shook her head with annoyance. "But I can't live with him any longer. I haven't told him yet, but I can't. I swear I can't get that girl out of my mind, and the possibility that she could have gotten pregnant by him only makes it worse. How many more women has he slept with?"

"But you don't know if the baby was Eric's. No one knows."

"That's not the point. It could have been his."

Autumn began to feel guilty, seeing that Lacy was so unhappy. "I'm sorry, Lacy. I don't know what to say. Do you still love Eric?"

"Not as much as before he cheated on me. I don't trust him anymore. I can't even believe anything he says to me. How can I continue to live with him?" Lacy started to cry, and Autumn sat next to her.

"I hate seeing you so miserable, but I think if you two stay together you can work it out. It takes time. You have to grow back together again."

Lacy wiped away the tears. "That's easier said than done. It's too bad between us now." She laid her head on Autumn's shoulder.

"When are you going to tell him?" Autumn asked.

"This week. I've got to get it over with."

"I don't understand. You're sleeping together but you don't want him anymore?"

"I know it's confusing, but I thought sleeping together would help make our marriage strong again. But it hasn't. I've made up my mind. I have to tell him." She heard a car and went to the window. "It's no one coming here."

"What if he goes back to that same woman again? Have you ever considered that he might? If he doesn't run back into her arms, other women will be waiting. You said that you made him the man he is, and he's a good-looking man, has a decent job, and he's intelligent, too. Other women will thank you for making him that man. They will thank you even more for making him leave."

Autumn looked at Lacy's face and by her expression, Autumn was certain that she wasn't ready to see her husband with another woman. "Have you told Mom yet?"

"Hell, no, and I don't intend to. Please don't tell her."

"I wouldn't. I went to see Mom and Dad and she was in the kitchen cooking dinner. Dad walked passed her and slapped her on the butt. Can you believe that? I've never seen him do that before. Looks like that vacation was exactly what they needed.

Whatever they did, it should have been done a long time ago."

"I've never seen him slap her on her ass either. I can't even picture it. When we were kids, I used to see him kiss her on the cheek, or place his hand around her shoulder, but no other romantic gestures. Mom didn't tell Dad to stop?"

"No, as a matter of fact, she giggled when he did it. Now back to Eric. Would it bother you to see him with another woman? You know that Jordan will see her, too. She may even be younger than you, and have his baby."

"Well thank you, Miss Marriage Counselor, for all this important information," Lacy snapped. "But I've thought of all the women he can get, and I still think our marriage is over."

Autumn stood up. "Are you crazy, Lacy? You need to give it more time. I know he hurt you, but you should give him the chance to make it up to you. Good men don't come by the dozen these days."

"He can't make it up, and he's already tried, and so have I. I can't trust him, so what kind of marriage could we have together? I have to do this; I have to end our marriage."

"Okay. You know what you're doing."

"Now that we've discussed it, I think tonight would be as good a time as any to tell him. Prolonging it any longer isn't helping. Tonight or next week wouldn't make any difference."

"Are you going to file for a divorce right away?" Autumn grabbed her purse and folded it under her arms. Then she opened the box of See's candy that was on the coffee table and started on the chocolate cream.

"Yes, of course I will. Why wouldn't I? I wouldn't try and clean him out by taking everything we've accomplished together. But I want the house until Jordan is eighteen. I can pay the note by myself."

Autumn noticed that even in Lacy's unhappy state of mind, there wasn't a string of hair out of place. She wore a navy-blue jogging suit and looked as though she had just stepped off the cover of *Vogue* magazine. Her makeup was flawless, the same color as her jogging suit, which looked expensive.

"I have to go and correct some school papers but first I have to stop at Albertson's to buy food to restock my empty refrigerator."

Lacy stood up to walk Autumn to the door. "Are you still planning to buy a house?"

Autumn nodded. "Yes, but I wanted one in a gated community. So now, I don't know where I'm going to buy." She thought of Matthew. They had planned to get married and she would have moved into his house in Hollywood with him. Now she had no idea where she wanted to buy. Her life had become so uncertain. She ambled to the door, and Lacy followed.

"Call me tomorrow if you need someone to talk to," Autumn said.

"Thanks. If I feel like talking I will call. Don't tell Mom. I don't want her running over here pissing me off by trying to tell me how to live my life."

"I won't," Autumn replied.

The sisters embraced, and Autumn sauntered outside. Lacy stood in the doorway and watched her until she drove off.

Autumn thought of Lacy all the way to the supermarket in Culver City. She knew that Lacy had made up her mind, and no one could convince her to change it.

It was nine-thirty, and Jordan was asleep. Lacy was in the living room waiting for Eric to come in from the kitchen. He had been on the phone for forty minutes talking to his sister who lived in San Diego, and waiting was making Lacy nervous. She just wanted to tell him and get it over with.

Finally, Eric hung up the phone. Lacy had told him that they had to talk. She looked sad enough to cry, and he wondered what had he done this time. She was never happy anymore. In recent weeks, she seemed to be pulling away from him. He was losing her, and he'd tried his best to get her back, but to no avail.

"Can I get you anything?" Eric asked as he entered the living room with a bottle of beer in his hand.

"No thanks. I'm all right. How was your sister?"

"She just wanted to say hello and find out if we were all right." He looked at her as though he were asking, but Lacy dropped her eyes to delay answering him.

Eric sat on the sofa next to Lacy so that he could face her. He wanted to see her face while they talked.

Lacy took a deep breath. She felt as though he was suffocating her. Why couldn't he take a seat in the chair opposite her?

"I'm waiting, Lacy. What is so important for us to talk about?"

"It's about us, Eric. We haven't been able to go back to where we were before you cheated on me. We can never go back, and to be quite honest, I'm tired of trying. We no longer have a marriage."

Eric knew she wasn't happy, but he didn't think that their marriage had fallen apart. He kept hoping that they could be the family they once were.

"I think if we gave it more time, you could love me again. I've never stopped loving you, Lacy. I know that I hurt you, baby, but you need to give us more time and try harder." He reached for her hand but she got up before he could touch her.

Lacy looked down at him; the hurt written across his face was heartrending. She didn't want to hurt him. "Eric, I'm sorry. I really tried for all of our sakes to keep our family together. Don't you think I wanted to see our son happy? It's too late. I can't get past the cheating, and I don't trust you anymore. How can we build a marriage where there is no trust? I don't even believe what you tell me anymore. If you're thirty minutes late, I wonder if you're with another woman."

"I didn't realize that you were so unhappy. But I still don't agree that it was all my fault."

Lacy sat up straight in her chair. "Well, who cheated, Eric? Who was seeing someone else and lying about it? It sure as hell wasn't me." She folded her arms over her chest and held her head high. The nerve of him to blame her for his infidelity. "You sat here and told me you cheated, and it's my fault?"

"You are so righteous, and you're never wrong about anything. It's your way or no way at all. How can I, or anyone for that matter, please you, Lacy? Even now you can't take any part of the blame. I love you, but if you can't change, then maybe you are right. We should divorce."

She was shocked at his attitude, and how easily he made it for her to end their marriage. Did he really still love her? "So you agree that we are finished?"

He stared at her as though he had to think of an answer, but it was only one answer that he could give her. "I don't agree that we shouldn't give it more time, and I don't agree that our son should live in the home without a father. I don't want him to be another black male growing up with one parent. But I will see him as much as I can, and I will make him understand that I'm always here for him. But I can't force you to love me again. I can't force you to grow up and realize life isn't perfect and you're not either." He'd forgotten that he had the bottle of beer and picked it up off the table. Eric took six swallows before he sat the bottle back on the table again.

"So, I was thinking of keeping the house until Jordan is eighteen. I sure wouldn't want to sell it now."

"Poor fellow. He's going to be confused enough. First I move out, then back in, and now I have to move out again. I wouldn't think of leaving and selling the house, too. First he has to get used to me not living here. He was so happy when I came back home."

"I know he was. But it can't be helped."

"Lacy, it can be helped. You don't want to give it enough time so you could heal. No one is picture perfect. You better change if you want to keep a man." He stood up.

"Wait, we're not finished."

"Yes, we are. Tomorrow I'll start looking for an apartment. As soon as I find one I'll move out. You can file for a divorce anytime you want. I'll sleep in the room with Jordan until I move." He got up and walked out the door.

Lacy sat with her mouth open. Did he really love

me? Was he giving up so easily? She leaped up off the sofa and followed him into Jordan's room. Eric lay on the other twin bed with his eyes closed. Jordan was asleep.

"You don't have anything to say?" She stood in the doorway.

"About what?"

Lacy looked as though she was flabbergasted. "About us, of course," she snapped.

"No. You don't want to be married to me, so we should get a divorce. I've tried, but apparently it was too late, and I won't kiss your ass any longer. Now, if you don't mind, I'm tired." He closed his eyes and heard her huff as she turned on her heels and rushed away from the door.

"Your house is beautiful. I wanted to buy one and was disappointed when I found out that I was too late. It's so beautiful.

"Yes, they are. I went to see one with a friend that I work with. He bought one, too."

Autumn sipped her wine, and placed her napkin back on her lap. "How long have you lived in Walnut?" she asked.

"Five years now. How is your steak?" Philip asked.

"Delicious. You cook a mean steak, which is why I ate so much. You are a really good cook, but I can't eat another bite."

Philip sat across the table from Autumn. She looked lovely in all black. The blouse was cut low and fell off her shoulders, her hair was pinned up in back, and her looped earrings dangled as she turned her head. Philip knew before he got her out of her clothes that he would kiss and caress her smooth shoulders. He loved her so much and couldn't be around her an hour without making love to her. It was hard to keep his hands off her, and tonight would be special.

Philip got up from the table and led her to the sofa. He couldn't wait any longer and held Autumn's hand in his. "Autumn, we've been dating for six months and I am totally in love with you."

"I'm in love with you, too, Philip." She looked in his eyes, and he looked so serious. She wondered what he was trying to say.

"Baby, will you be my wife? I'll be the best husband that you could ever imagine. I know how to love and appreciate a woman."

It was as though the world stood still, and they were the only two alive. After Matthew, she didn't think anyone would ever love her enough to propose marriage again. She knew that Philip was different. He was a dream come true.

Autumn felt tears on her face, and Philip kissed them away. "Yes, yes. I will marry you, Philip."

She watched as Philip wiped a tear off her face, then gathered her into his arms. He was so easy to be with and talk to and so easy to love. She felt as though she had met him before. Autumn wanted him to make love to her. In the past, she wanted everyone, but Philip was the only man she loved. She wanted to marry him and wanted to have his child and be with him for the rest of her life.

"You know I will be a good husband don't you?" He pulled the ring from his shirt pocket and slipped it on her finger. The diamond sparkled; from the size of it, she knew it was expensive. Autumn held her hand up. "It's so beautiful, Philip. You shouldn't have."

"Oh, yes. I want to give you the best."

"You are my one and only love for the rest of my life."

"Promise?" Philip asked.

"Yes. Promise."

"You still want one child?" he asked.

"One, maybe even two."

"Do you really mean it, Autumn?"

She kissed his lips, and tasted the wine. "For you, love, I would have two children. But we'll see after the first one." Autumn laughed at the thought of babies running around their home.

"Where do you want to live? I thought since you teach in Compton, and I work in LA, I could sell my house and we could pick one out together." He had been thinking of it all week, assuming that she would accept his proposal.

Autumn listened with a smile. He had thought of everything. "You don't mind selling your house and moving to LA?"

"No. That's where you live." He raised her right hand against his lips. "I would move to another state to be with you."

"Would you go to my parents house with me next Sunday? My mother will be so happy when I give her the news."

"Of course. It's time I meet your parents again. It was so brief at church the first time I met them. It's time you meet my dad, too."

They talked and made plans for the future, but they couldn't keep their hands off each other, and after an hour had passed, Autumn helped Philip place the dishes in the dishwasher, and they made their way to Philip's bedroom. Autumn stayed overnight, leaving the next morning and going straight to her parents' house.

"Mom, you are going to love him," Autumn said with excitement, and held up her hand so Betty could see her ring.

Betty gaped, and held her hands to her mouth. "Oh, honey, you're engaged?" Betty asked gleefully. She was ecstatic. "Autumn, I'm so happy for you." She touched the diamond on Autumn's finger. "You are a lucky woman. I knew the first time I saw him that he was a decent man, and the Sunday he took you to breakfast, I prayed that you two would get together. I'm telling you, it's good to know that one of my daughters is happy. Sit down and I'll make us a cup of tea. I bought a new flavor at the store yesterday." They were in the kitchen, and Betty grabbed two mugs from the cabinet.

"Have you talked to Lacy today?" Autumn asked.

"Yes. I spoke to her this morning."

"I feel guilty for being so happy when she's so depressed."

Betty set the mugs on the table and dropped a tea bag in each one, then filled the cups with steaming water. She took a seat and sipped her tea. "Now, don't you dare feel guilty, Autumn. You deserve to be happy. Honey, it's about time you find a good man to treat you well. Heaven knows you've been through enough misery."

"Thanks, Mom. I started to call her yesterday but I felt too bad to."

"So did I, but I decided to give her a few days. Eric is moving out tonight. This time I'm going to let Lacy take care of her own business, and without me. I almost lost your father by sticking my nose every place but where it should have been, and that was here with him."

"I'm happy to hear you say that. It's about time you and Dad are happy together and going on trips. But I never thought of Eric cheating on Lacy. She can't get over it. One day she'll find a man who can satisfy her."

"Men stray sometimes, Autumn. But Eric came back and you know how hard Lacy is to please. She may not ever find a man to make her completely happy." Betty thought of her own marriage. She knew that Emmit had cheated on her, too. But he'd come back to her. She hadn't mentioned it to him, but she knew there was another woman. She could feel it every time she looked at him, or every time he stared aimlessly. She didn't ask, because she couldn't endure the truth. But she knew. Now their marriage was as solid as a rock, and she intended to keep it that way. "Lacy will have to learn that no one is perfect. Not even her," Betty said.

"Amen to that," Autumn commented.

" Now, tell me what it is that you like most about Philip."

Autumn didn't have to try and think of something. She knew exactly what she loved about Philip. "He's easy to talk to, and he's like someone who you knew for a long time and fell out of touch with, then you meet again, mend the relationship, and everything just falls back into place again. And you know what, Mom; he always wants to please me. Philip admires me for teaching school in Compton. With Matthew, his career was the only one that was imperative."

"Matthew was selfish, that's all. What should I cook for dinner next Sunday? I want to cook something that Philip likes."

"Cook whatever you want, Mom. He'll eat it." Autumn stood up. "It's time I go home, but at least I don't have to correct school papers tonight. I finished at work today."

"Your father will be home soon."

Autumn headed for the door. "Tell Dad that I'll see him on Sunday." When Autumn got to the door, she stopped and turned around to face Betty again. "Does Dad ever say anything about the life I lived a few months ago? Sometimes I wonder if he has forgiven me."

"Emmit was angry with me for keeping it a secret, Autumn. He was never angry with you. If I hadn't kept it a secret, somehow he believed that he could have protected you. But that was my fault because I didn't tell him. Now I realize that I was wrong. He had a right to know. Are you still going to your meetings?"

"Sometimes, but I'm so much better than before. I have my confidence back and I feel strong and determined to be the person I was before I got ill. I wonder if Dad has any respect left for me."

All Betty could do was gather Autumn in her arms. "Of course he has the same respect and love that he's always had for you. He realizes that you were ill."

"Okay, Mom. Tell Dad that I will see him next Sunday." She strolled out the door.

Betty stood at the large window and watched Autumn walk to her car. Dressed in her olive-green suit and pumps, she looked very sophisticated. Betty smiled; her daughter was a lovely woman. But just as easily her smile disappeared as her thoughts suddenly shifted gears. She thought of Lacy and how unhappy she must be. Betty looked at the clock; it was five-thirty. Emmit would be home soon.

* * *

Lacy went to Jordan's room as Eric carried boxes back and forth to his car. Jordan had been crying and wanted Eric to stay home. He couldn't imagine his parents living apart and sharing him. He threw his body across the bed. It was all his mother's fault. She was breaking up their family. He'd overheard their conversation early that morning and knew that it was her.

"Would you like some ice cream, Jordan?" Lacy asked. She sat on the edge of the other twin bed watching him. It was breaking her heart to see her son so sad. She watched with wide eyes as he quickly jumped off his bed, his feet dug into the thick carpet, and wiped the tears off his face.

"Why are you making my dad leave? I want to live with him. Not with you." He turned his back to Lacy.

"You can't live with your father, but you can spend the weekends with him."

"Can my dad spend weekends with me here?" he asked with a hint of hope in his voice as he faced Lacy.

Lacy hesitated before she answered him, but he had to know. She didn't want to hurt Jordan. "I'm sorry, Jordan, but it doesn't work that way. Dad can't spend the weekends here with you. You'll have to go to his new apartment. Your dad and I love you very much, honey."

Jordan's eyes were red with tears and his small face twisted into a frown. He took one step away from Lacy. "I hate you, and I don't want to live with you." He stomped out of his room and went to plead with Eric one last time. He had to make one last ditch effort to hold his family together.

Lacy was so heartbroken that she couldn't move.

Jordan was hurting, but he was only a little boy who didn't understand. All she could do to help him was give him all the love and attention he needed. It was as though he knew their lives would change forever.

Lacy heard Jordan crying, and heard Eric trying to explain that leaving didn't mean they wouldn't be together again. She, too, felt tears burn her eyes. What had happened to their lives, their marriage that other couples had been so envious of? Eric's mistakes were breaking their son's heart. Lacy got up, wiped her tears, and entered the living room, where she found father and son sitting on the sofa. Jordan's head was resting on Eric's shoulder. She wondered if Eric realized it was all his fault.

Lacy sat next to Jordan, and he looked up at her. His mother touched his arm, but he snatched it away from her.

"Jordan, don't be nasty to your mother. Both of us decided to get a divorce."

Jordan held up his head. "I heard her when she said that she didn't want to be married to you anymore. I had to go to the bathroom and I heard her, Dad. I hate her for making you leave."

"But you can see me anytime you want."

"It's not the same. Nothing will ever be the same again. This is why kids run away from home. And I'll run away, too." Jordan got up and ran to his room. As Lacy and Eric looked at each other, they heard his door slam.

Eric felt responsible for everything. If only he hadn't cheated. But for days he wondered if their marriage would have lasted very long even if he hadn't.

Chapter 16

Autumn slipped into a pair of jeans. She had regained the weight that she'd lost and looked good in her jeans again. The doorbell rang, and she looked in the mirror one last time, grabbed her purse, and went to welcome Philip.

He gathered her into his arms. "Hey, baby. I see you're ready." He kissed her lips and held her hand.

"Yeah. My mom is tickled pink. She probably has been cooking since she woke up this morning."

"Well, let's go. I could use a good home-cooked meal."

They chatted as Philip drove. "It's time we go house hunting," Philip suggested.

Autumn turned so she could see his face. "What area?"

"The Westside. What about Culver City?"

"There are some beautiful homes off Overland, around Ranch Boulevard," Autumn said.

"That's a start. What about next weekend, and after we look we can stop by my dad's house."

"Okay. Have you told him that we're engaged?"

"Yes, and he wants to meet you."

"Turn right at the next signal. Now make a left, and we're here," Autumn said. She was happy, and without a doubt she knew that she and Philip would be married.

She rang the doorbell and Emmit answered. Philip was standing just as tall as Emmit. Both men were over six feet.

Emmit kissed Autumn on her cheek. "Come, come in and make yourself comfortable," he said as he looked at Philip.

"Dad, do you remember Philip when we were at church, and he took me to breakfast?"

"Yes." Emmit and Philip shook hands.

"Is that you, Autumn?" Betty yelled from the kitchen.

"Yes, Mom." Autumn watched Betty as she walked into the living room. "I remember you, Philip. It will be nice to have a new man in the family."

"Thank you."

Emmit and Philip took a seat on the sofa, and Autumn followed Betty to the kitchen.

"He is better looking than I remembered. Dinner is already cooked, but it's only two."

"Dad is calling me. I'll be right back." Autumn went to the living room where Philip and Emmit were talking about the basketball game.

"Honey, bring me and Philip a bottle of beer, please."

"Sure. Be right back." Autumn went back to the kitchen. "They want a bottle of beer."

"Okay. Everything is ready so I'm going to the living room and have a seat. Besides, I want to get to know my future son-in-law."

Autumn and Betty went back to the living room and Autumn sat next to Philip; Betty sat in the chair. She wanted to know everything about the man whom Autumn was going to marry.

"Philip, I hope your family is as happy as I am about you and Autumn getting married." Betty said.

"My mother isn't living, but my dad is pleased. I'm taking Autumn to meet him next weekend. He'll fall in love with her the moment he sees her. I know I did." Philip squeezed Autumn's hand.

"Is Lacy coming over today?" Autumn asked.

"No. She and her neighbor are taking the boys to the Pomona fair. I'm sure once they leave, Lacy will want to go straight home," Betty said.

They chatted, and Emmit turned on the television to watch the Lakers play basketball. At four-thirty, they had dinner, and Autumn went back to the kitchen to help Betty with the dishes.

"I like him, Autumn. He has values, and I can see how much he loves you every time he looks at you. And you love him, too."

"I do, Mom. Sitting next to him today, I realized that he has helped me more than the meetings, or the counseling. He's been my rock."

They went back to the living room. Philip looked at his watch.

"Are you finished in the kitchen, Autumn?"

"Yes, and you have to drive all the way back to Walnut."

Philip stood up and shook Emmit's hand again, and kissed Betty on the cheek. "You are the best cook I know, Betty."

Betty smiled. "You're such a charmer. But I want

you to come back whenever you need a good meal. I cook every Sunday."

Emmit and Betty stood on the porch and watched as Philip's black SUV turned the corner.

"Now, there goes a real man, Betty. He'll be good to Autumn. I won't have to worry about her anymore." Emmit felt relieved now that his daughter would be safe.

"Your parents are nice people. I'm sure that my dad and your father will get along well." Philip felt a cool breeze sweep across his face. He smiled as he glanced at Autumn's black wind-blown hair.

"What's your dad like?" Autumn inquired.

"I'm a lot like my dad. He's one of the good old dudes. He's understanding and patient, and he never judges others. As a matter of fact, he's been waiting for another daughter-in-law." He smiled as Autumn blushed. "I'll have to take him to meet Emmit and eat your mother's good cooking. That woman can sure bake a good blackberry cobbler."

"Well, we'll just have to take him to visit my parents. My mom loves to cook for people who she thinks enjoys her cooking. She'll have dinner ready whenever you go to her house."

He glanced at Autumn whenever he could. It was hard not to look at her. Her cheeks were no longer sunken, and she was now the perfect size. The first time he saw her in the church, he thought she was too thin for his liking. She was pretty when she smiled, with exquisitely sculpted, fine features, perfect teeth, and dancing dark eyes; but she was so thin.

Philip parked in front of Autumn's apartment building, walked around to the passenger's side, and opened the door to help her out. They walked hand in hand across the street.

Autumn unlocked the door to her apartment, and they went inside. Before she could drop her purse, Philip grabbed her and gave her a long, passionate kiss that made her legs weak.

"I've wanted to kiss you all day," he whispered softly against her ear, then kissed her neck, easing his free hand under her sweater in the middle of her back.

"I hate it when you have to get out of my bed and drive to Walnut."

"If we go to bed now, I can get up and leave about five in the morning. That's staying all night in your bed," he said with a teasing glint in his eyes.

"Well, I should get you in bed early. It's six o'clock," she whispered between kisses.

They walked hand in hand to her bedroom. Once they were there, pieces of clothing led a trail to the bed.

He made love to her slowly, savoring every stroke, every touch, and the taste of her made him wild with hot passion.

"Oh, you make me feel so good," she said tantalizingly, streaking her fingers down his back and buttocks, feeling his body arch into hers. She arched her legs higher, and heard him groan, then stiffen, and held him close, as close as she could. She didn't want to ever let him go, and she wanted him to stay in her life forever.

Sated, Philip rolled off of her and held her in his arms. He wanted to feel her body close to his. "I'm so in love with you, Autumn. Sometimes I wonder where you have been all my life."

"I, too, love." She gasped as his mouth fastened on

her nipple and tugged gently. His head rose to see her expression. "I'm glad you're here with me all night."

Philip pulled her even closer into his arms, and both fell into a slumber.

"Jordan, you have to stop this kind of talk. I'm your mother and I won't have it."

"I don't care if you are my mother. I want to live with my dad. I don't want to live with you anymore. You made my daddy leave me." He ran from the table to his room without touching his dinner. Lacy started to go after him but didn't have the strength to fight with him again. What could she do or say to make Jordan understand that it was not the end of the world. Funny, she thought, it was Eric who cheated and tore their family apart, but it was she that Jordan was angry at. It had been a week since his father moved out, and Jordan hadn't eaten dinner. At night, he stayed in his room and watched TV, and Lacy went to hers. At dinner he stared at his plate but didn't attempt to eat. When she asked him to eat he would refuse, cry, and say he wanted his dad.

Lacy got up and cleared the table. She snatched the plates up, rinsed them off, and angrily placed dishes inside the dishwasher. Lacy wiped off the table, and all the time she was fretting out loud to herself about the changes in their lives. She went to her room and grabbed the phone and dialed Eric's number. It rang three times before he answered.

"Hi, Eric." Before she could say another word, she heard him sigh heavily into the phone.

"Is Jordan all right?" he asked as soon as he heard Lacy's voice.

"No, I mean yes. Well, not really. He's having a hard time with the separation. You are going to have to come over tomorrow and talk to him. I thought by now he would at least be polite to me. He blames me for everything, and it was you who cheated. But of course he doesn't understand it." She waited for his answer.

Eric sighed again. "Okay. I'll be there as soon as I get off work tomorrow evening. Are you all right?"

"I will be once Jordan can tolerate being in the same room with me. Next week is my vacation. Maybe if I take him someplace and we do something together he might feel better."

That wasn't the answer he wanted, but he listened. "I'll be there tomorrow and have a talk with Jordan." The conversation ended as suddenly as their marriage had.

Lacy walked outside to the patio and felt a cool, balmy breeze against her face. She looked up when she heard rumbles of thunder in the skies; suddenly she felt sad and lonely. Her future was uncertain. She hadn't imagined that her marriage to Eric would end because of another woman. Would she get married again? If she did, how would Jordan react? She folded her arms against her chest and breathed in heavily. It was much too soon to think about marriage again. She had to concentrate on her son's happiness. She heard the phone and went inside. Probably Eric, she thought as she reached for the receiver.

"Hi, Lacy."

"Hey, Autumn. What are you up to?"

"I've just finished correcting papers. Have you been okay?"

"I've been better. Jordan is having a hard time with

his dad not living here. But Eric is coming over to-morrow evening to see him. I don't know what to say to make him feel better." She wiped tears from her eyes. "How's Philip?"

"Good. He was here last night, and this morning I might add." She smiled as she thought of their time to-gether. "We are going house hunting next weekend."

"Where?"

"Culver City, and the Westside."

"Sounds great." Lacy heard the happiness in Autumn's voice, and Betty and Emmit were finally happy together. She was the only one in the family who was uncertain of her future, and all of a sudden she didn't feel like talking to Autumn about her hap-piness. Lacy wanted to lock herself in her room and cry, but she couldn't. She wouldn't want Jordan to hear her. "Girl, how did you get Philip to ask you to marry him?"

Autumn pulled the phone from her ear and looked at it as though she was looking for an answer. For a moment she'd forgotten how nasty Lacy could be.

"Believe it or not, I'm good enough for someone to love and marry. I'm also good enough that he wouldn't cheat on me," Autumn snapped.

Lacy sat with her mouth open. How rude, she thought.

"'I have to go, Lacy." Without waiting for her to answer, Autumn hung up.

Eric had a damn good reason to cheat on her sister.

Just as he promised, the next day Eric was home to talk with Jordan.

Jordan ran from his room when he heard the door open and shut. "Dad, did you come to get me?" he asked and threw his body against Eric's.

Lacy walked out of the kitchen. "I have enough beef roast left over. Why don't I fix you and Jordan a plate? I have a report to go over and you two can be alone."

"So, what you say, Jordan?" Eric asked. He rubbed Jordan's head and danced around him as though he were a boxer.

Lacy watched from the kitchen. It just wasn't fair for Jordan and Eric to be so close. She always felt left out. The boy adored his father. But in spite of their differences, Eric was always a good father.

Lacy moistened her lips and placed a small bowl of salad in the middle of the table, then pulled two plates from the cabinet.

Eric decided he would discuss the problem with Jordan after dinner. He would talk to his son about school and make plans for the weekend before he brought the subject up.

"Dinner is on the table," Lacy announced, and went into the den.

"Everything looks great, huh Dad?"

"Yes, and I'm starving. I miss your mother's cooking." He glanced at Jordan to see his reaction, but the boy acted as though he didn't hear.

They chatted about school and the new teacher. "I wish Aunt Autumn was my teacher. Then I could do whatever I wanted to," he said with a mouthful of food.

"Oh no you wouldn't. You would do as you're told if she were your teacher. I'm sure she's a firm teacher." Eric enjoyed the dinner. He hadn't had a home-cooked dinner since he'd moved out; he stopped and bought fast food on his way home from work.

After dinner Eric and Jordan went to Jordan's room and closed the door. "Come here fellow and sit beside your old man. We have to talk. First, what do you want to do on the weekend?"

"I want to go to a movie," Jordan said, taking off his shoes. "Then what about ice skating?"

"Ice skating is good. I'm sure I can manage to skate, but not as well as I used to."

"Dad, can't you please come home. I know it's Mom's fault, but can't you come back home please?"

Eric placed one arm around Jordan's shoulder. "I know it's hard for you. But Jordan, life goes on. You can't go around the house saying mean things to your mother. It's not all her fault. We agreed to separate; both of us agreed." He watched as Jordan dropped his head.

"I miss you very much, son, but I wouldn't be happy if I stayed with your mother, and she wouldn't be happy either. Do you really want to see us unhappy?"

Jordan nodded.

"I know you are hurt and confused. Your mother and I are going to do everything to make you happy, but you have to do something for me, too."

"What, Dad?" Jordon hung his head down to hide the tears.

"You are the man of the house and have to take care of your mother, instead of treating her badly. You have to be my little man."

"Does she need me to take care of her?"

"Of course she does. You're the only man here aren't you?"

Jordan smiled. "I guess I am. But I didn't know that she needed me to take care of her."

"You two have to take care of each other. I'm depending on you, Jordan."

Jordan smiled as he looked up at his father. "Does she know that she needs me to take care of her?"

"Of course she knows. That's why you have to treat your mother with love and respect. You treat every woman with respect, Jordan. Always remember that."

Jordan nodded again. "I'll remember, Dad, and I'll take care of Mom."

"Okay, I'm counting on you." Eric stood up. "I have an early day tomorrow, but the weekend will be just me and you."

Jordan looked at his father with his big brown eyes and smiled. "Who will take care of Mom while I'm gone on the weekend?"

"She'll be all right. One weekend away is all right. Come on, walk me to the door. I have to say good night to your mom." They walked hand and hand to the den.

Lacy gave Jordan a close look and saw no tears. For a change, he actually looked happy.

"Jordan and I have come to an agreement. He's going to take care of you while I'm away."

"Is that true, Jordan?"

"Yes, Mom. You need me to be nice and take care of you."

"Is it all right if I pick him up Friday evening instead of Saturday?"

"Sure, Friday is good," Lacy answered with a wide smile. She was relieved to see a smile on her son's face. Lacy got up and went to the living room with Eric and Jordan. Eric was walking to the door when he heard Lacy call his name.

"Thank you, Eric. I really appreciate you coming over today."

"I appreciate the dinner. See you in two days,

Jordan." Eric walked out the door and Lacy went back to the den.

"I'm sorry that I've been so mean to you, Mom." He laid his head on his mother's shoulder.

"It's all right, Jordan."

Chapter 17

"Now, Autumn, don't forget to water my plants."

"Mom, the last time you and Dad were away, I came over every day and put your mail inside the house and watered your plants. I won't forget."

"Okay, honey. I would ask Lacy to do something but she would forget, or so she would say that she'd forgotten. You know how your sister is."

"Yes, I know. How bad is Aunt Irene?"

"Henry said she had the stroke yesterday and she can't talk. She even sleeps with one eye open. I hope she's not paralyzed permanently."

"It's six o'clock here, so it is eight in Texas. Dad seems to be taking it pretty well." Autumn could see him from the living room. He was on the phone talking to someone from Dallas, Texas, and was inquiring about his sister's health.

"He's really worried but he'll never admit it. You know how your father is. Never let anyone know how he feels, but I know the man. He's worried all right."

"You're almost ready, Betty?" Emmit asked. He came into the living room with his hat in his hand.

"Yes. And I hear the taxi driver blowing his horn," Betty answered.

Autumn helped Emmit carry the luggage outside. Before Betty got inside the car, she kissed Autumn on her cheek. "I don't know what I would do without you, Autumn."

"Woman, get in the car," Emmit insisted.

Autumn laughed and shook her head. She went back inside and closed the drapes, took one last look around the house, and locked the door.

It was Saturday morning and Autumn was up early. She and Philip were going house hunting. She had a bowl of oatmeal and cup of coffee. When she finished, she took a hot shower and slipped into a pair of black jeans. She went to the living room and waited for Philip. But as soon as she sat on the sofa, he was ringing the doorbell.

Autumn opened the door; Philip smiled and gathered her in his arms. "I love to see you in your tight jeans."

"I just love seeing you. Have you eaten?"

"Yes. I had a ham and egg sandwich before I left. I got up early and went to get a paper, then bought my sandwich." He grabbed her arm. "Come sit down for a minute. I want you to see this house in Playa Vista. And there's one in Westchester and in Culver City, too."

"Okay." She followed him to the sofa. He gave her the newspaper. "All three look nice."

"Which one do you want to see first?" Philip asked.

"Culver City. It's on Ranch Road and it's very nice over there."

Autumn got her purse and jacket and they left her apartment.

Philip parked his car in front of the two-story house in Culver City. The realtor was having an open house, so they didn't have to make an appointment to see it.

"It looks nice," Philip said.

"Yes. I like the neighborhood, too. It's clean and quiet."

They were the first ones who had arrived. The realtor greeted them and started a tour through the house. "Just take your time and look at this beautiful, very well-kept property. My name is Miss Wilcox. Just call me if you need further assistance." She went back into the living room and started flipping through papers in her briefcase.

"I love the kitchen tile. What do you think, Philip?"

He looked at Autumn's face and she looked happy. He could envision her cooking dinner in the kitchen, and a child's footsteps tottering through the house. Looking at her was evidence that she loved the house. "I like the house, Autumn. If this is the one you want, we can buy it."

"But wouldn't you want to see the other two?"

She wanted this house, he knew. And he wanted her to be happy. "I love this one, but if you would rather see the other two, we can."

"No, Philip, I love this one, too." They went to the master bedroom. "It's perfect for us. I love the house inside and out," she said anxiously, as she peeked through the window and saw another couple walking around the back of the house.

"So it's settled?" the realtor asked.

"It's settled," Autumn and Philip answered in unison, then looked at each other and laughed.

"You've made a good choice, and you've certainly made my job easy today." She was a tall woman, standing over six feet tall, and she had dark hair. "Here, why don't we take a seat at the table and complete a Purchase Contract." Philip wrote a five-thousand-dollar check for the deposit.

Philip and Autumn talked about the house all the way back to her apartment. As they stepped inside, Philip gathered her into his arms. "It all seems so real, baby." He kissed her tenderly.

"It's real, and it feels good. Want a cup of coffee, juice?"

"I'll take coffee. The cup I had this morning tasted like black shoe polish."

"I'll have one, too," she said. She went to her small kitchen and Philip sat at the small table and watched her.

"I like the house much better than the one that I selected before. Maybe it's because we did it together. It's larger, and it belongs to both of us," Autumn said.

"I'm looking forward to us moving in together. I went alone to buy my house, but I didn't want to go alone again. It's a house for a family."

"Yes, I agree. A house for our family, Philip."

"How are your parents?" he asked.

"They left yesterday. My aunt had a stroke, so they rushed off to Dallas, Texas. She's my dad's sister."

"I'm sorry to hear that."

Autumn placed his coffee in front of him, but he didn't say anything. He watched her dancing eyes, her soft smile as she sat opposite him. Her eyes were happy, not at all like the sad eyes of the woman that he'd first met. "How long are you going to make me wait?"

She tilted her head to one side; she looked as though she was going to speak but didn't. Instead, she poised like a hummingbird in midair. She wondered why she always felt as though they'd known each other forever. Autumn reached over and hooked her fingers into his. "What am I making you wait for?" she asked with a teasing glint in her eyes that he'd seen so many times before.

"You are making me wait to marry you, and I want to very soon."

Autumn smiled, and touched his face. The times they had together were always so peaceful, and they were so good together, reading each other's body language, each other's thoughts, and loving each other unconditionally. "Okay, let's come up with a date."

"Do you have a calendar?" Philip asked.

"Yes, I'll go and get it." She hopped off the barstool and went to her room. She was back in two minutes and placed the calendar on the counter in front of him.

"Do you want a big wedding? After all, it's your first marriage."

"No. I'm not into big weddings. Besides, we could use the money for our new house. Just family and a few friends is enough for me. My closest friend moved to Europe a year ago." Autumn hadn't thought of Terra during her recuperation in the hospital after being beaten up. Terra had left only four months before all of that, and Autumn didn't tell Terra because she would have had the added expense of coming back to Los Angeles. "I sure miss her. I went to help her get settled in. She teaches, too."

"Will she come for the wedding?"

"She would for me, but I won't tell her until after we're married. She just bought a new house, and coming here would be another added expense."

Together they looked at the calendar. "It's October now, and my mother died on New Year's Day. What do you think about New Year's Day?" Philip suggested.

"I think New Year's Day is very special. Yes, it's a good day for us to get married on. It will always be special to us, Philip."

He wanted to hold her in his arms forever, to thank her for her thoughtfulness and understanding. "Living together will always be special for us, Autumn." He held her hand in his.

"I have to go to my office and work on a proposal for Monday morning. Would you like to come along?"

"Thanks. But I need to go shopping and work on a project for the children so I can have it ready for Monday."

Philip stood up and took Autumn's hand to lead her to the door with him. Then he kissed her again until her legs were weak. Feeling her firm breasts against his chest made him want her, and he sighed heavily. "I better get out of here before we end up on the sofa, or the floor. My dad is anxious to meet you tomorrow. We are going to have a wonderful life together, Autumn."

"I know we are." She watched Philip stride briskly out the door and was amazed at the loneliness she felt as he drove off into the streets. In three months, she would be married.

As Autumn walked out the door to go shopping, she thought of what a lucky person she was. Her life had gone to hell and back.

* * *

Lacy arrived at the coffee shop on Centinela and Beach Avenue in Los Angeles at precisely 1:00 PM. She had seen the place before but never had any reason to stop there. Michael Watson, a new member of the Chamber of Commerce of Westchester, California, was going to meet her for lunch. Michael was so good-looking, so refined, and intelligent. Now he was a real man, Lacy thought. He was perceptive and had noticed everything about her. They had met only three weeks ago, and he could sense that she was unhappy. At the last meeting, Lacy overheard a woman asking someone if he was married. But when he stood up to introduce himself, Michael didn't mention anything about a wife. He did say that he owned a company that Lacy wasn't familiar with.

Lacy had tried to convince Eric to become more involved in the community, but he'd declined, always having an excuse. He was involved only in the Little League for Jordan and was complacent with the life they led. So she thought, until she found out about his little cheap affair. But Michael was a man who had seen the world. He said that he traveled a lot, ran his own company, and invested wisely.

Lacy watched Michael park his blue Mercedes Benz across the street. He was dressed handsomely in a pair of brown slacks and a white sweater.

She pulled her mirror from her purse to see if her hair was still intact. She stuffed the mirror back inside her purse and waited for his entry.

Michael kissed Lacy on her right cheek. "I like this place. It's not fancy but I meet my clients here, and the food is excellent. So how is your day going,

Lacy?" He flashed a dazzling smile that made Lacy's heart ache and her blood run hot.

"It's good, and yours Michael?"

"Now that I'm here with you, terrific. I went to my office and tightened up loose ends with an apartment building that I sold. Had I mentioned that my office was in Westchester, too?"

"No. But I assumed it was since you're a member of the Westchester Chamber of Commerce."

"I share my office with my sister. She was still working when I left."

"How long have you been in real estate?"

"Eight years, and we have done very well, too. You looked sad last weekend, but today you look happy. Is that because I'm here?" He touched her hand and looked straight into her eyes. He knew that she wanted him, and he sensed that she was lonely. He could always tell when they were lonely and hot for a man.

Lacy's heart throbbed as Michael held her hand. It was hard to believe a man who looked so good and had so much going for him was single.

"What are you doing the rest of the day?" he asked.

"I don't know yet. My son is with his dad this weekend, and I feel lost. Maybe I'll go shopping."

"You're not one of those ladies who get depressed and then spend too much money are you? My sister does it all the time."

"Oh, no." She didn't want him to know that if they got together, he would be spending his money on her, too. Although she loved expensive gifts, he would find that out later.

"Are you ready to order?" he asked.

"Yes. I'm starving." She looked at the menu and decided on the Cobb salad and Coke.

"I think that I want the steak. You can do better than a salad, Lacy. Get a steak, live a little."

She sat back in her chair. A man after my own heart, she thought. "Okay, I'll take the steak."

Michael ordered for both of them. "After we finish lunch, we can go someplace quiet so we can be alone. I had my eyes on you from the first time we met."

"What do you mean someplace where we could be alone? I was just meeting you for lunch." She was humiliated. How dare Michael think that she would jump in bed with him because he bought her a steak.

"I thought you were lonely and needed some male companionship. But don't get upset, we can be friends and have a good steak dinner and go our separate ways."

"You thought that I was lonely and looking for a man?" Lacy sat straight up in her seat. She was so embarrassed and felt so mortified that he had gotten the wrong impression of her. How could she have been so foolish?

"Look Lacy. We got off on the wrong foot. Why don't we talk about our jobs or family. Really, there's no need to get all uptight. Just a little misunderstanding, that's all."

"Okay. Maybe I'm jumping to conclusions. I'm sorry that I gave you the impression that we would sleep together."

The waitress came with their lunch and they started eating and talking again.

"This was a very interesting day. First, one of my deals fell through, but I closed the other one. Now you are going home to a lonely house, when you could be having fun while your son is away."

Lacy started to get up and walk out, but she didn't want to create a scene. Instead, she forced a smile and nodded. "It's not like that, Michael."

"But, baby, why not? We can become so close. I'm a good man, Lacy, and I like you. Give me a chance to show you."

Lacy closed her eyes to clear her head. She had had enough of this jerk. This so-called man of the world.

"So you aren't going to change your mind?"

Lacy grabbed her purse, and started to get up.

"Wait. I'll pay the bill and we can go out together." He patted his pockets, stood up and patted the back. "Damn, damn, damn. I forgot my wallet."

"What! You, what?! I'm stuck with the bill?"

Their table was close to the door, and it was forced opened so hard and fast that Lacy and Michael could feel the force of the wind from it.

"You two-timing bastard. I saw your car while I was driving. You are supposed to be at your office with a client," the woman said. She looked older than Michael, and very angry.

"Who is she?" Lacy asked as she jumped out of her seat. She was shocked; her eyes were wide and with questions.

"I'm his wife. Now who the hell are you?" The woman turned to look at her husband. "Don't tell me she's your client, or I'll go off right here and now on both of your asses."

"Oh, Lord, what have I gotten myself into?" Lacy asked, and sat back in her chair again. She had never been so humiliated.

"Come on, Michael."

"Baby, let me explain." But before Michael could say another word, his wife hit him over the head with her purse. Then she turned around to face Lacy. "If I see you with my husband again, I'll kick your ass. Cheap sluts like you always breaking up married mens' homes."

Lacy opened her mouth, but the words were stuck in her throat. She looked for Michael to help, but he was already at the door, and his wife went yelling behind him.

Lacy looked around and everyone had stopped eating; they were staring and laughing at the scene. She pulled two twenty-dollar bills from her purse, placed them on the table, and rushed out of the restaurant. Once she was outside and in her car, she whispered out loud to herself, "What had just happened?" She was unable to comprehend what had happened so fast. One minute she was eating her lunch with a total jerk, and the next minute his wife, whom she knew nothing about, was threatening her. Confused, she drove off fast. When she parked her car again, she was in front of Autumn's apartment. She didn't know how she got there, but she was. She held both hands in front of her, and they were still shaking.

Autumn was rinsing the cups and placing them in the dishwasher when she heard the doorbell ringing. She grabbed the dishtowel and dried her hands as she rushed to the door. She was surprised to see Lacy standing there.

"Can I come in?"

"Of course you can." Autumn stepped aside and closed the door. "Why do you ask?"

Lacy held her hand to her chest as though she was out of breath. "Because I've been such an ass lately. I wasn't sure that you would want to see me."

"Yeah, I agree. So what else is new?" Autumn was standing with one hand on her hip, but Lacy walked past her and took a seat on the barstool at the kitchen counter.

"I guess I deserve that. The coffee smells good."

"I'll get you a cup." Autumn looked at Lacy as she placed her purse on the counter. Were her hands trembling? Glancing out of the corner of her eye, Lacy placed both hands against her temples.

"Do you have a sinus headache? The air is bad out there today."

"It's not because of my sinuses, but I do have a headache."

"Then what?" Autumn placed the cup of coffee in front of Lacy, then perched on the other stool. She was prepared to hear about the argument that Lacy obviously had had with Eric. "Okay, what did Eric do this time?"

"Eric? This is not about Eric. I went on a luncheon date with a guy today."

"Was it business?"

Lacy sipped her coffee. "No, but it was innocent. He's a new member of the Chamber of Commerce. I needed someone to talk to. I needed to know that a man could still find me attractive. So when he asked me to lunch, I figured what could go wrong? I didn't think he was married because he wasn't wearing a ring on his finger." She stopped and closed her eyes.

"Go on, don't stop now," Autumn urged enthusiastically.

"Well, as it turned out, he thought we would have lunch and then a nice little roll in the hay afterward. After I set him straight, he conveniently forgot his wallet. I'm telling you, everything happened so fast. I felt as though I had stepped into the twilight zone."

"So you paid for his lunch and then came here?"

"No, not exactly in that order. We were sitting at a table close to the window. His wife came in like a roaring tornado."

Autumn shook her head. "Does it get better?" she asked with interest.

"Yes. She was loud, angry, and embarrassing. She said that if she caught me with her husband again, she would kick my ass. Everyone stopped eating to watch the show. It was shameful. I mean really shameful. Just wait until I see Michael again."

"It's crazy out there. You have to know who you are dealing with or you can get hurt, Lacy. You can't tell the good people from the bad. Don't have anything to do with that man again. And please believe me, you're not the first woman that he has played around with."

"You're telling me. Do you have any Advil? My head is killing me."

"Sure." Autumn went to the bathroom and came back with the bottle in her hand.

"Do you want water or juice?"

"I'll take water. I found out one thing today. I am not ready to date. I just don't want to start the bullshit and lies all over again." She held her hands up in front of her; they had stopped trembling. "So, what are you going to do today?"

"Philip just left before you got here. We looked at

a house in Culver City and both of us loved it. And we also decided on a wedding date," Autumn beamed.

"Good. What day did you decide?"

"New Year's Day."

"That's pretty special. I'm happy for you, Autumn. Really I am. You've had so much sadness in your life, and I want the best for you."

Autumn looked deeply into Lacy's eyes and believed her. Her sister really wanted her to be happy. The phone rang and she answered.

"Hi, Mom. Everything is okay here. Stay in Texas as long as you need to."

"How are my plants, Autumn?"

"The plants have been watered, and the trash cans are in the backyard, so don't worry about anything here. Okay, call me next week and let me know." Autumn hung up.

"I'm going shopping. It may make me feel better," Lacy said getting up.

Autumn watched Lacy until she got inside her car. Maybe someday Lacy would find as much happiness as she had.

Autumn looked in the mirror one last time, and went to the living room to wait for Philip. It was Sunday, and she was going to meet Philip's father. Philip had tried not to appear too anxious, but she knew that he was. She was beginning to know him quite well. She sat back on the sofa and closed her eyes and visions of their new home came to her. They would be happy there, and the backyard was great for a child to freely run around and play. Autumn had no doubt that they would have a happy life together.

The doorbell rang, and her heart skipped a beat. Philip had arrived. She opened the door.

"Are you ready, sweets?"

Jack lived alone in a small house in Windsor Hills off La Brea and Northridge Boulevard, in Los Angeles. He was a tall man, with gray hair. Jack greeted Autumn with a warm smile and patted his son on his back as they took a seat in the living room. The furniture was antique. Autumn was sure that it was purchased long ago.

"Dad, this is Autumn Evans," Philip said.

"Welcome to my home, Autumn. Can I get you something to drink? 7-Up? Beer?"

"Beer for me, Dad," Philip said.

"I'll take the 7-Up," Autumn answered. She watched Jack as he left the room. "Your dad is as tall as you are."

"My uncles and my brother are tall, too. But my mom was only 5'3," and small. People used to ask her how she had large boys like us. When I was a kid, I hated being the tallest in my class."

"I know. A girl in my class is the tallest and she hates it, too."

They chatted for hours, and Autumn told Jack about her family and her teaching. She wanted him to meet her parents, and have some of Betty's good cooking, and he agreed. Since his wife had died, he did the cooking for himself.

"You can bring a date if you like," Autumn suggested.

"Thank you, maybe I will. I just might do that." Jack was sixty-four years old and had been dating the same woman for six years. Her husband had died five years before she'd met Jack, and they cared deeply for each other.

As Autumn looked at him, it was like looking at Philip. He smiled every time he looked at Autumn.

"When is the wedding? Don't wait too long, son. You better grab this one and hold on to her." Jack thought his son was a lucky man. Autumn was intelligent and very attractive. She held her head high with dignity. Too bad Susan couldn't have lived to meet Philip's second wife. She hadn't liked the first one.

"We're getting married in three months, Dad. New Year's Day." Philip couldn't wait to tell him the date. He saw his father wipe a tear from his eye. Father and son looked at each other and knew instantly what the other was thinking. Susan had died on New Year's Day.

"That's pretty special, son. New Year's Day is a good day to add Autumn to our family." Jack had lost his wife, but he would gain a daughter-in-law.

"We found a house yesterday. It's not far from here," Autumn said.

"It's in Culver City, Dad, with a big, nice backyard."

"A big backyard is good for children," Jack answered.

"We plan to have a child. Maybe even two," Autumn interjected.

Jack beamed. He was happy with their decision to get married. It was obvious that they were in love. He had been waiting for a grandchild.

"Where is the restroom?" Autumn asked.

"Go down the hall and make a left," Philip said.

Jack watched Autumn as she ambled away. "She's kind of thin, son. She needs more weight on her, and you want her healthy if she's going to carry your babies."

Philip laughed. "She has gained weight. Autumn was thinner when I first met her. But now she's just right for me." Her curves were distributed in all the right places for Philip. When he saw her naked, he couldn't keep his eyes and hands off her.

Autumn came back to the living room and took her seat back on the sofa. They chatted for another hour.

Philip stood up. "Well, Dad, I wanted you to meet Autumn. I'm happy that we have your blessings."

"I'm happy too, but I'll be happier when I see my grandchild."

Philip took Autumn's hand and they started to the door. Jack opened the door and kissed Autumn on her cheek. "You are always welcome to come here anytime. My house is always open to you."

Autumn folded her arms around Jack's neck. "Thank you." She kissed his cheek.

"Come on before you two make me cry," Philip said.

Philip and Autumn said good-bye and left Jack standing in the doorway watching as they got inside the car and drove off.

Chapter 18

They sat in her living room. "The dinner was good," Autumn said. They had left Philip's father's house and stopped and had dinner before arriving at Autumn's apartment.

"Yes, it was. I was just thinking of my dad. He was happy to meet you and he does want us to get married and have a child."

Autumn laughed. "He made it clear that he wanted a grandchild. But so do my parents. They only have one grandson."

"You know, we should start practicing tonight," Philip teased.

"I'm still on the pill, but we can practice so when I'm off it won't take too long." She gave him a wicked smile.

Philip took Autumn's hand and led her to the bedroom. She giggled all the way.

Once in her room, he undressed her slowly, watching every inch of her lovely body. The fires started as soon as they were undressed and in bed. They were made for each other, knew what the other needed and wanted.

Philip watched her face as she was on top. He loved watching the pleasure in her eyes and reached up to run his fingers through her hair as he moaned when she pushed down to get more of him. He pulled her down and got on top of her. Then he held her legs high and firmly, with deep strokes, gave her all he had.

Autumn held on as Philip held her closely to him, his hands on each of her hips, and as she closed her eyes she heard him whisper, "Do you want me, Autumn?" He held her tighter, held her legs high, held her hips as he went deeper, deeper inside her. "Do you want me, baby?"

"I want you, Philip." She whispered the words over and over again. Then like a flash of lightening, she saw the face, heard the words, and recognized the hold he had on her. It was Jeff. God, it wasn't Philip. It was Jeff, the man she'd met in the bar, the man who'd taken her to the Marriott Hotel in Marina Del Rey. The same man she'd dreamt about, the man with no face. How could it be? So many times she felt as though she knew Philip in another life. How could he have done this to her? Had he been laughing at her all the time? She felt dizzy, as though the room was spinning, and her life was spinning out of control. What must he think of her, and why would he even want to marry her?

Autumn pulled away, jumped out of bed, and grabbed the blue bathrobe. "Jeff," she screamed. Her hands flew to her face, her eyes wide and frightened, and her body trembled from the chill in the air. She felt cold, so cold that she held her robe tightly around her.

Philip froze. He'd wanted to tell her so many times,

but it was never the right time. After time had passed, it made no difference, and he loved her. He was convinced that she would never remember him. He had to make her understand how much he loved her.

He got out of bed and slipped into his jeans. "Autumn, let me explain. It's not what you think. I love you, baby, we are going to be married." He reached out for her, but she pushed his hands away.

"No, no," was all she could manage to say. Other words were stuck inside her throat. She shook her head from side to side and held up both hands in defense.

"Autumn, it's not a game. We've selected the home; we're going to have a family together. You've got to forget about that night and get past this. Think of what's real now," he pleaded.

"We are not getting married, and we are not going to have a family. Now I know why you didn't want to know about my past, you already knew it. Everything was only a game to you. How you must have laughed at me," she shouted, and began to cry. "When were you going to ask me?"

Philip was standing a few feet from her. "That day at church, I didn't remember you. But the next day, I realized that you looked familiar to me. Still, I didn't know it was you."

"When?" she screamed. "When did you realize that it was me?"

"Two weeks later; but I liked you too much by then. I just figured that you were unhappy about something that night. You were drinking, and your eyes were so sad. I'd never seen anyone with such sad eyes before. But even then I knew that you were a special woman. What difference does it make how we met? As far as

I'm concerned, the first time we met was at the church concert." He was standing and took a step closer to her. "Give me your hand, Autumn. We can work this out."

Autumn took two steps backward. She needed some space between them. "I want you to leave, Philip." She took off his ring and tossed it on the bed. "I want you to leave now. Nothing can ever be the same again between us. I can't trust you."

"You don't mean it, Autumn. How can you turn your back on all the plans we've made? I have never judged you. The only thing I'm guilty of is not telling you. I still love you. One night doesn't make a difference to me. I haven't asked you any questions about the night we met, because it made no difference to me."

"I'd rather you had asked questions. One night I was raped and beaten because I'm a damned sex addict. I was looking for a man to sleep with the night I picked you up." She stopped when she saw the muscles in his face drop, the shock in his eyes. She had seen the same in Matthew's eyes, the same disgust and accusation. It was all there, all over again. She had to weather through another heartbreak and disappointment of what she had become, and another man that she loved with all her heart and soul. She wasn't at all sure that she could do it again without dying.

When she saw that he was too shocked to answer, she spoke first. "It's over, Philip. Please leave."

Philip stood in shock, feeling numb. He never thought of her having sex addiction. He always thought that she'd had too much to drink that night, or maybe she had just broken off an engagement with her lover, but never a sex addict. He looked at her as though she were a stranger.

Autumn couldn't bear to look at his face. She knew that he hated her. He wouldn't want her now that he knew. She was angry, but now she was hurt, torn in pieces, fed up, and tired. How long would she have to live with the curse?

Philip finished dressing in silence and started out the door. He turned around to look at Autumn once more, but her back was turned to him. He walked out the door, not saying good-bye. He was too hurt and disappointed, and most of all, he still loved her.

When Autumn heard the door close behind Phillip, she collapsed to the floor and cried out loud. Minutes passed before she got up and went to the bathroom, pulled out the bottle of sleeping pills, and went to the kitchen to get a glass of water. She twisted off the cap, counted ten pills. Her hands started to shake, then she threw the pills against the wall. What would killing herself prove? What would it do to her family? It would stop her from feeling the hurt, but it would kill her parents. What she had to do was stay home and suffer alone, no man to sleep with, no wild, hot sex. She had to beat the curse, live clean, or another beating would kill her.

She went back to her bedroom, took a pillow from her bed, and went to the sofa. Autumn turned off the lamp and lay on her back in the darkness, the stillness. She wouldn't go out; she would fight it. She waited, she waited, she waited.

Late into the night Autumn was still awake. She cried and prayed for sleep. And finally, when she had no tears left and her eyes felt like marbles, sleep took over mind and body.

She woke up at six the next morning and made herself a strong cup of black coffee. She went to the bathroom to brush her teeth and wash her face. She pulled the bottle of eye drops from the medicine cabinet and dropped two in each eye. As she stared at herself in the mirror, she said out loud, "I did it, I did it." She had no sexual desires coursing through her body or ordering her to go out. She was hurting like hell, but she was free, her body and soul were free and clean. *I stayed home last night, alone.*

Philip tossed and turned all night. "Sex addiction, sex addiction," he heard the words over and over in his head. He never would have known, but he couldn't blame Autumn. She had tried to tell him, but he refused to let her. He had almost forgotten the night they met. He lay on his back and closed his eyes. How could he have been so stupid? She never asked him to answer "Do you want me?" since they'd started dating, and she never said it to him again. He wondered why was it so important for her to hear it the night they met. Maybe she needed to feel wanted. And he did want her.

It was six when Philip crawled out of bed, but his head hurt like it had been hit by a baseball bat. Too much booze last night, but it was the only way that he could sleep. Philip went to the bathroom and stood under the shower, but his mind was still on Autumn. He loved Autumn, and still wanted to marry her. She had to know that; he had to make her know. If only she would listen to what he wanted to say, and what did he do so wrong anyway? It was she who had wanted to have sex. He would have settled with sending her home in a taxi. Now he understood why she was alone in a bar. After he'd gotten to know her well, he wondered more than once why she was alone the night he met her.

A month had past and Autumn still refused to see Philip or answer his phone calls. He had lied to her, and now that he knew the truth, she was sure that she had lost him. Their relationship was built on a lie. He hadn't called her over in a week, and she was sure that her problem with sex addition had sunk in. He no longer wanted her, but the only man she craved to have sex with was Philip. Her life again was only teaching.

There was no place in her life for another man, not one who would want a woman who was a sex addict. She was astonished that she hadn't remembered Jeff—or was it Philip?—or whatever the hell his name was. The entire situation was horrendous when she thought of it, and that was every day and night. She woke up with Philip on her mind every morning and weathered through the day without him, thinking of all the plans they had to live the rest of their lives together, the family they were going to raise. She loved him and had lost it all.

It was late that evening and Autumn had just finished correcting papers and was working on a project for her students. She neatly stacked the papers in her brown leather briefcase and set it on the coffee table. She started toward her bedroom when the doorbell rang and she stopped. She wasn't certain if she should answer it or not, but it rang again, then again. Autumn sighed and ran her fingers through her hair to try and look presentable. It had been over a week since Philip had called her and Autumn wondered if it could be him at the door. Had he come back to her? Could he marry her knowing what she was?

Autumn opened the door and looked up at his face. He was smiling down at her.

For moments she was speechless and felt as though she had awakened out of a dream. "Hi, Matthew. What are you during here?"

"May I come inside, Autumn?"

She forced her body to move aside, then closed the door behind him.

"Can we sit down?" he asked, and started to the sofa. Autumn sat next to him.

He looked staid and comfortable, as though he'd never left her. "You look good, Autumn."

"Thanks. But you haven't answered my question. What are you doing here? The last time that you were here, you hated me."

"If only I could have managed to hate you. Every time I thought of you lying naked next to another man I wanted to hate you, but I couldn't. I'm sorry that I didn't go to the hospital to see you when Lacy called. But I was so hurt and angry."

"Yes, so was I," she said, feigning a cringe. Just the thought of that night made her sick.

"Are you still ill?"

"I no longer pick up men if that's what you're asking." She tried to keep her voice even, without trembling. But seeing him was too painful. The last time she saw Matthew he was so cold and angry. She still remembered the hatred in his eyes and the harsh words he spewed out at her.

"You mean you haven't had any urges to go out at

all?" He reached over and held her hand in his, but she gently pulled it away from him. She wasn't ready to get close to him. He was the stranger whom she thought she would never see again, and she'd gotten used to not having him around.

This time she turned around to face him with more confidence than she had the night he walked out of her life. "No, Matthew. I haven't had any urges for strange men. Not that it should matter to you. You told me how you felt."

He looked in her eyes and was taken aback by the chilliness. "It has always mattered. Autumn, I've been dating a woman but it's not serious between us."

"Why not, and why should you be telling me this?"

"Because I've missed you . . . us. I miss what we had together. We made so many plans for our future."

"What about your career? You wouldn't want one of the surgeons to see you with someone like me."

He noticed that she had grown cold, and he had so much to make up to her. "That doesn't matter anymore. All that matters to me is that you forgive me."

For a second she closed her eyes and saw Philip's face. He was the man whom she had planned to marry and have a family with, but he was the man who had lied to her. She loved him, and he didn't tell her the truth. And for some reason, Matthew thought he could come back into her life as easily as it was for him to walk out of it. But he had never lied to her. She had hurt and lied to him. She was confused and tonight was too soon for her to make a sensible decision. She needed time to think. Everything was moving too fast.

"I'm going to be honest with you. I just broke off

my engagement to another man. I was going to be married and need time to think and clear my head."

"How long has it been?"

"A month."

"May I ask why?"

"I think not, but it's not for the same reason that you walked out on me."

He deserved a better answer from her, but he could sense that she was angry with him. When they were together, she wasn't honest with him. "Are you still in love with him, Autumn?"

"I don't really want to talk about it." She saw disappointment written all over his face. Did he really think she would wait for him to come back into her life after he left her? It wasn't any of his business how she felt about Philip. "I need time to think about you and me. I'm not sure how I feel about you anymore."

"I know how I feel about you. My feelings haven't changed." But as he looked at her, he wasn't sure if she would take him back. After all she had done to him, she should be thankful that he would even consider taking her back. Matthew stood up. "I won't rush you, but this time I won't let you go so easily. I still love you, Autumn." He kissed her on the cheek and started to the door when he heard her call him. Matthew turned around to face her.

"Did you ever wonder what shape I was in when Lacy called to tell you that I was in the hospital?"

"Of course I wondered if you were hurt badly, but she didn't call me back so I figured that you were all right." But he was too angry to care. "Were you hurt badly?"

"It doesn't matter now." He nodded as Autumn

watched him close the door. Well, she thought, this was certainly a turn of events.

Autumn went to bed around ten, but she didn't get very much sleep. Her thoughts went from Philip to Matthew, only Philip hadn't called.

The next day Autumn was summoned to the principal's office, and a teacher's assistant stayed in the room with her students until she came back.

"Hi, Diane. Is everything all right?" Autumn asked as she took a seat in front of the desk.

"Yes. Take a seat, Autumn. I have some great news for you. I got a call this morning from the school district. You know how all the parents praise your work with the students?"

"I try to do a good job. Besides, I love teaching. As long as I can remember I wanted to be a schoolteacher."

"Well, I'm going to retire. My husband is ill and he needs me at home. I recommended you for my job. If you are interested, you go before the board next week. I'll stay with you for a month if you accept. I know that you can do it and are the best person for the job. You really care for the children. Another principal may not care as much as you do. And this being a low-income area where the parents work long hours, some of them on drugs and some children with only one parent at home, the kids need a principal who cares."

"I am truly honored to be considered for the position, and I love it here. I wouldn't think of teaching at any other school."

"Then you should take the job. You've been qualified

for it for a long time. It's just that it wasn't available before now."

"What about Joyce. She's the vice principal. I don't want to step on anyone's toes."

The phone rang. "Let me get this call," Diane said.

Autumn was facing the window and saw the children playing. She looked in the corner at the large green plant that she had bought for Diane's last birthday. She hadn't ever imagined that one day this office would be hers. She couldn't wait to call her mom with the news of her promotion.

"That call was the order for the supplies. Anyway, Joyce wasn't offered the position because she and her family are moving back to Dallas, Texas, in three months. You'll be busy hiring another vice principal and a teacher to replace you."

Autumn smiled. "Okay, I'll take it." The job was just what she needed to boost her confidence again. She didn't do well with relationships, but she would do well by helping the children. It was all she had left.

Chapter 19

"The man fell in love with you, Autumn, and was afraid to tell you," Betty said, counting the pieces of mail that had accumulated when she and Emmit were in Texas. "My goodness, you would think that we were away for months. In my opinion, you are taking it much too seriously. Men marry prostitutes all the time. He knows you're not one of them. You met a man in a bar and went to bed with him, so what's the big deal. It's not the nicest thing you've done, but people do it all the time. It's not a crime, honey. The worst thing is that damn Matthew running back to you with his tail between his legs."

"Matthew wants to come over every night, but I won't allow it. I still can't get over the fact that he didn't come to see me when I was in the hospital. Not even a phone call."

"Well, keep that in mind. Philip loves you, Autumn. But Matthew, he loves Matthew."

Betty and Autumn were sitting at the kitchen table with two tall glasses of apple juice. "I'm sure that Emmit will agree that he likes Philip, too."

"But Matthew and I have a history together. We know each other's moods, needs, and habits. We had planned a life together." But Autumn had to admit that she and Philip were always so relaxed together, and being with him was so peaceful. Being with Matthew was always a challenge. Either with their careers or where they would live when they got married. It was a day-to-day challenge. Everything had to sparkle with Matthew. If only Philip had told her that they had met before, in a bar, and gone to a hotel to have sex that she'd advocated. It sounded revolting, but it was the truth of the matter. It was what she had done, what she had wanted. And now that the reality had sunk in, his phone calls had stopped.

Matthew knew what she was, and he'd come back. If she didn't marry him, she was sure that no man would ever marry her. She thought of the beautiful house that she and Phillip had selected together, the day he came to the school where the fair was being held. Matthew had never gone to the school because of the location. It was in Compton. He wanted her to teach at a school on the Westside. Compton school district wasn't good enough for a woman that he would marry. But still, he wanted to marry her. No one else would. Not even Philip.

Autumn stood up with her purse in her hand. "I'm going home. I had a long day today." She hadn't been sleeping through the night for weeks.

"You should stay. Lacy and Jordan are coming for dinner."

"I'll be back on the weekend, Mom. I'm too tired today."

"Okay, but you think about what you're doing. Please don't let Matthew rush you before you give the situation some deep thought. I really thought you and Philip would be planning your wedding, and here that smart-ass Matthew comes back into the picture."

"Mom," Autumn laughed. "I know it's not funny. It's mind-boggling, and I don't want you to worry about me. Matthew is all I have left. Philip doesn't call me anymore."

"When you have a child of your own, you are going to worry, too." Every instinct she possessed told her that Philip was a better man.

Autumn kissed Betty on the cheek and sauntered out the door, hoping she would get home before dark. Since the brutal beating, she hated being out alone after dark.

As Autumn unlocked the door the phone began to ring. It rang three times and stopped on the fourth ring before she could answer. She flopped down on the sofa and sighed, laid her head back, and closed her eyes. Five minutes later, the doorbell rang. When she opened it, Matthew was there, wearing a wide smile that made her heart skip a beat. But she wasn't sure if it was the excitement of seeing him or if it was that she had gotten used to him not being there. He kissed her fully on the lips and she accepted it. By his long, hungry kiss, she knew it wouldn't be long before he'd try to make love to her, but she was in no hurry.

Matthew followed her to the kitchen. "Do you have anything cold to drink? I feel as though I'm de-hydrated. It's the long hours I've been working."

"Have a seat. I have some cranberry juice. You got me hooked on the stuff."

"It's better than your Pepsis." He took a seat at the kitchen counter.

Autumn set two tall glasses in front of him, and

got the large bottle of cranberry juice from the refrigerator. She started to fill the glasses when the phone rang. It was Lacy.

"Hi. What's up? Sorry I didn't wait for you at Mom's house, but I was tired."

"Autumn, tell me you are not seeing Matthew again. Did you forget that he didn't even see you when you were hurt? That jerk said he never wanted to see you again."

"Everyone makes mistakes." Autumn turned her back to Matthew, hoping he wasn't listening to her conversation.

"You sound as though he's there."

"Yes, you're right. How's Jordan?"

"He's good, and congratulations on your new position. Principal, girl you should feel good. We have to talk about Matthew later, and I won't take no for an answer."

"I just know you won't, and thanks. I am very proud to be promoted to principal. I'll stop by your house tomorrow." Autumn hung up the phone, and sat next to Matthew. It almost felt like old times again. Almost.

"Baby, did I hear you say that you were promoted to principal?"

So he was listening. "Yes. I still can't believe it myself. I've been on cloud nine since Diane asked me. She's taking an early retirement to take care of her husband."

"Diane?"

Autumn looked at Matthew's face when she thought she heard disappointment in his voice.

"Yes, Diane. Aren't you happy for me, Matthew?"

"As a matter of fact, I'm very disappointed that you

would accept the position as principal in Compton. You are smart, and a damn good teacher. But to accept the position is totally incomprehensible to me when there are schools on the Westside."

Her happiness deflated immediately, and her eyes flared at his insult. "The children need me, Matthew. I thought you had gotten over the idea that teaching in a better district makes a better teacher. Don't you know that the schools in Compton, and farther east don't get the best books or supplies that are needed? The school is mostly Black and Hispanic, and they need me. Our kids deserve better," she explained with a distinct edge in her voice. Silence fell between them as she felt tears burning her eyes.

"I'm sorry if I hurt your feelings, Autumn. I just want the best for you. You have so much to offer and you could climb the ladder faster if you were in a better school distinct." He was a doctor and wanted to be proud to introduce her as the principal of a school in Windsor Hills, or El Segundo, California. But he would drop the conversation for the moment. He would demand that she transfer to another school district after they were married. Matthew stood up and pulled her into his arms. "You look a little tired."

"I am. I haven't been getting very much sleep."

"Why? Could it be that you are overly excited about me coming back? I would stay with you to-night, but I'm on duty till 7:00 AM tomorrow. You didn't answer me."

"About me being overly excited? I don't know, and I have a lot to learn before Diane leaves. I'm a little on edge." Feeling better that he had to leave, Autumn forced a weak smile. The tension had gotten too thick.

"I can go out and buy you some dinner."

"No. You go home and get some sleep. What time do you go on duty?"

"Eleven, but I'll call you before I leave to hear that beautiful voice."

"Or to make sure that I'm home?" She sounded hurt.

"No, of course not." He looked down at her and kissed her again. "I saw a house for sale in Baldwin Hills. Why don't we meet tomorrow so you can see it? I'm sure that you will love it. I sure do."

She had to compose herself before answering. "You seem to have already considered buying it before we had the chance to select a house together. Were you afraid that I would want to live in Compton, too?" she asked, trying to keep her tone carefully neutral.

"Have I made you angry by trying to make life a little easier for you? I shouldn't have said anything because the house was going to be a surprise. It's your wedding present from me. As always, I want to make you happy." He gently took her hand and held her close.

"I'll let you know if I can meet you tomorrow." She walked him to the door. All of a sudden she wanted to be alone.

Once they were at the door he placed one arm on her shoulder. "Get some sleep. I hope you're in a better mood tomorrow. We've wasted so much time, Autumn. I'm ready to marry you so we can start a life together."

Autumn nodded, and watched him walk out the door. She went to her room and lay across her bed. She had changed and didn't like the fact that Matthew was making all of the decisions. Funny how she wasn't aware of it before. When he first left her, she was unable to eat or sleep without crying over him. She dreamt of him coming back to her, prayed for the day that he would. But now she realized how selfish he really was. So why did she still love him? She got up, undressed, took two aspirin, and got into bed.

Autumn lay awake in the dark, thinking of her new position. She wanted Matthew to be happy for her, but instead he made her happiness dissipate into thin air. Why wasn't she ever enough for him? But still, he was the only man who would marry her. With her new position, and Matthew back in her life, why wasn't she happy? She had cried for Matthew night after night and finally he'd come back. So why was she so miserable? And it hurt like hell when she thought of Philip. She turned over in bed and sighed. Another sleepless night, she thought.

The next morning Autumn was up early and in her classroom before seven. She was awake at dawn and couldn't go back to sleep, so why stay in bed? Besides, being at work kept her busy. And before she realized it, it was past eight and time for the children to line up to come inside.

The day went just as fast, and Autumn left at four. She promised Lacy that she would stop by on her way home.

"Come on in," Lacy said as she held the door open for Autumn to come inside.

"Do you have a Pepsi?" Autumn asked.

"Sure do. Take a seat and get comfortable." Lacy went to the kitchen and came back with two Pepsis. "Now, let me talk some sense into you, girl. What do you think you're doing?"

"Trying to get my life back."

"But you had it back, and better than before. Do

you still love Matthew?" Lacy asked with a perplexed look.

"Yes. I never stopped loving him."

"Then why were you going to marry Philip?"

"I was in love with Philip, and I didn't think that Matthew would ever come back to me. We belong together."

"I've seen women talk about the men they love with a glow on their faces. You look grim, Autumn. You just got the perfect position, you are going to marry Matthew and you couldn't look more unhappy. You better think about what you are doing."

"Philip lied to me."

"So did Matthew."

"What do you mean? Matthew has never lied to me."

"Yes, he has. He said that he loved you, but you could have died, and where was he? I called him and he didn't even ask if you were all right. Years from now, you are going to regret marrying him. Besides, he's too phony. He wants to be more than who he is."

Autumn just looked at Lacy. She knew that Lacy meant well, but who was Lacy to call someone else phony?

"I can't tell you what to do, but one day you will have to admit that you are still in love with Philip. I hope you do before it's too late."

"What about Eric?"

"It's over with us. I've filed for a divorce, and I'm not doing too badly. I lost all faith in Eric. I've always been true to him, and never once thought about cheating. I tried to stay in the marriage, but I couldn't. When you can't trust someone, you lose respect. He's a terrific father, and I will always love him, but it's over."

Autumn set the Pepsi can on the coffee table in front of her and slipped out of her shoes. "Are you ready to date?"

"Not after that last episode, and we weren't even dating. I'm not ready yet."

"You know, some days I do want to talk to Philip. We were so perfect together, and I was sure that he was the man that I would marry," she said with a faraway look in her eyes and stopped in mid-sentence.

"Autumn?"

"Yes?"

"Do you believe that Philip doesn't feel the same toward you since he knows who you are? But he knew who you were when he asked you to marry him, and it didn't make a difference then. So why now?"

"It may later on in years if we got married."

"I don't think so, Autumn."

"He stopped calling me," she said, and wiped a tear from her eye.

"Maybe he thought that you couldn't forgive him. Give him a call, honey."

"I can't."

Lacy leaned forward. "Why?"

"I can't face him. He knows what I was, and I can't face him. Matthew knew, and I didn't have to call him. He came back on his own."

"Matthew knew what he lost. Who else would tolerate his phony, selfish ass but you? You adored the man."

"I can't look at Philip, and I don't think that I can stand the way he might look at me. He would always remember how we met. I'm surprised he even introduced me to his father."

Lacy pointed at her head. "Hello up there. When you two were falling in love, he was looking at you, and he knew who you were, Autumn. The man fell in love with you."

"The fact remains, he stopped calling me. What can I do? I have some pride you know. I can't lose what little pride he left me with. I'll never forget him." She felt miserable just discussing Philip. For a short while, he was her dream come true. The memories of their lovemaking, all the laughter they'd shared, and planning their life together; now she felt as though she were dying inside. It was easier to think of Matthew.

"What happens when Matthew gets angry with you and throws it back in your face? He will, you know."

Autumn looked as though Lacy had thrown a glass of cold water on her. It hadn't occurred to her that Matthew would throw her past back at her, but it was very possible. It was more than possible, it was an actuality. Oh, God, she hadn't thought of it. Matthew was already disappointed with her for accepting the position as principal for the Compton school board. What would it take before he reminded her of the life she'd led? No, if he were going to marry her, he wouldn't be that malicious. Could he, she wondered?

"Autumn?"

She looked at Lacy. "Did you say something?"

"I called your name twice. Are you all right?"

"No. I mean yes." She stood up. "I'm tired. I need to go home and get some rest."

"I'll get you a plate to take home. I cooked enough

in case you wanted to stay and have dinner with me." She looked at Autumn's face again before she left her alone. By the worried expression on her face, Lacy wasn't at all sure that Autumn and Matthew would be getting married. But Autumn was still in love with Philip.

Philip sat in his car after he went for the last walk-through inside the house that he and Autumn had selected together. He sat there thinking of Autumn, and the house they were supposed to move into together to have a happy life. He decided that he would buy the house. After the escrow closed, then what?

As Philip drove off, he thought of the first night that he'd met Autumn in the bar. As she came inside, all heads turned. He couldn't keep his eyes off her. She looked so beautiful, so sexy sitting at the bar.

The next time he saw her was at the church concert but he didn't recognize her. She looked vaguely familiar, but she had gotten thin and didn't smile through the entire concert. In the beginning of their relationship, and he did recognize her, it only made her more intriguing, and he was curious as to why she was in a bar alone. Inside the bar, it was she who'd picked him up, but at the church concert it was obvious that she was a lady. Not at all the woman he'd met the first time. He even wondered if she had two personalities, the woman he met in the bar and the one in a church. But the first personality didn't appear again.

Lately, Philip started reading about sex addiction, and now he understood her shame and humiliation. He realized her anger for having an illness that she had no control over, and one that could ruin her reputation as the decent woman and teacher she actually was. If only he could tell her that it didn't matter. He loved her as she was now and hadn't forgotten her since the first time he set eyes on her.

Would she come back to him? He was still in love with her and wanted her back in his life. But he wouldn't push her. He would give her the time she needed to think things through, and she would realize that they were made for each other. In time, Autumn would realize that no other man loved her as much as he did.

Philip drove his car into the driveway of his home in Walnut, California.

Chapter 20

The weeks passed fast for Autumn. Diane had left and she was now the principal, with additional responsibilities. A new teacher had filled Autumn's vacant position, and the students would come to her office to see her every opportunity they got. Their new teacher was nice, but the children wanted Autumn back.

Autumn arrived home with her briefcase heavy with work. Matthew was waiting for her and got out of his car as soon as she placed the key inside the door. They went inside together.

"You said that you would be home at four, and it is already five-fifteen," he said, exasperated, and looked at his watch. He followed her to her bedroom where she placed her purse and briefcase on the dresser. The tone of his voice stopped her, and she turned to face him. "I told you that I would try and be home around four."

"Your coming home late has been going on for weeks, Autumn. You are taking this new position of yours too seriously. What about our wedding plans? We haven't even spent a weekend together." Before she could answer, he stormed out of the room and went to the kitchen.

Autumn sat on the edge of the bed, her head hanging low, and her spirits dampened. She sighed and pulled off her jacket and slipped out of her shoes.

When Autumn went to the kitchen, Matthew was sitting at the counter with two tall glasses of cranberry juice. She sat opposite him.

"What would you suggest we do about the situation? We both have hectic careers, though mine won't always be," Autumn said.

"I don't understand how it's going to get better for you with those underproduction, underprivileged kids in Compton," he snapped. "They are always going to need extensive time that will be taken from us. You're principal of the school now. Why can't you appoint someone else to do the work so you can leave on time?"

Autumn glared at him in disbelief. "Do you care for anyone besides yourself, Matthew? Is this the way it's always going to be, having me please you with no regard for anyone else or anything that I want? I can't live this way," she said and turned her back to him. Autumn sighed and closed her eyes. Philip would never put her through such unhappiness. He wanted her to be happy. Oh, where did that come from? It seemed to just bolt from the blue.

Matthew stood up and grabbed her hand. "Baby, I'm sorry. I'm just so used to it being just you and me. Our schedules are so crazy right now, and I missed you this week." He gathered her into his arms and kissed her.

Autumn wondered if he missed her when they were apart. She laid her head on his shoulder and felt tears on her face, closed her eyes, and Philip was there. He was always there confusing her, making her unhappy.

Because she was late getting home, Matthew couldn't stay long. He had to go on duty at nine at the hospital.

While Autumn was at work the next day she kept busy, busy because she was implementing new ideas in the computer of some of the slight changes she'd made that would increase the school budget, busy because it prevented her from thinking of the disruption in her life. The phone rang. Autumn answered, her right hand inadvertently moving to her mouth. "I'm fine, Philip, and yourself?"

"I'm all right. But I miss you terribly. I think of you every day."

Autumn just held the telephone; her heart beat like a drum. "I'm so sorry about the way we parted, Philip."

"You broke it off. I didn't want to call off the engagement. I really do love you, and I hope that one day we can go out to dinner and talk about it, or maybe one day we can start over again."

"Do you mean like we just met for the first time?" she asked hopefully.

"If it would make matters easier for you. As for me, I'll settle for getting married, and getting you pregnant." He chuckled softly.

In spite of the shock from hearing from him, Autumn had to smile. "Maybe, one day we can talk about it."

"I hope so. I don't want to push you, but I'm here if you want me. Good-bye, Autumn."

"Philip?" She was too late; he had hung up. She clicked off the cell phone and placed it in her desk. He said that they could talk one day, but she felt the need to talk to him sooner, much sooner. She was engaged to marry Matthew, but she wasn't happy. What had happened to the days when she was so happy and honored to marry Matthew? When he left her she could barely breathe, and her heart was ripped to pieces. She closed her eyes and remembered how she would trace the small scar on Matthew's chin with her finger. Where had it all gone? Maybe she couldn't forget the fact that he wasn't concerned enough to visit her in the hospital. Didn't he care at all? She would have visited him if he were hurt. Autumn turned off the computer. She needed some air and went outside to walk around the school grounds.

That evening Autumn was home by four. Matthew arrived shortly after. She had changed into a green jogging suit.

Matthew was in a romantic mood and couldn't keep his eyes or hands off her. He kissed her in the kitchen, and before she could get to the living room he was kissing her again. "This is what I missed, Autumn. Remember the way it used to be between us? I want that again. We've been too busy." He gently pulled her to the bedroom and down on the bed.

They kissed, and Matthew laid her on her back, pulled her pants down her legs. "You look so good," he whispered against her hair.

She needed him so badly that she began trembling for him. It had been too long. She watched Matthew as he undressed and lay beside her. Her body was close to his as she felt his full, warm lips on her mouth. Hungrily, she returned his kisses, her mind fading into the heat of passion. Suddenly her eyes flew open, and she pulled away from him. "I can't do this. I'm sorry, but I just can't." She reached for her pants when Matthew grabbed her arm.

His eyes were dark and perplexed. "What's the problem, Autumn? I thought you wanted to make love as much as I did."

"I thought so, too. But I can't." She pulled her pants up her legs and stood up, grabbed her sweatshirt, then flopped down beside Matthew. He tried to pull her close, but she didn't budge. She needed the space; she needed to breathe and feel free again. She'd felt free and happy with Philip. But Matthew made her feel like a child who needed his approval for every decision she'd make.

Matthew dressed and watched her as she ambled back to the living room. What in hell was going on with Autumn? In the past she couldn't seem to get enough of him. Since her sex addiction was manageable had she lost her desire for sex? Or had she lost her desire for him? No, it couldn't be. She had to be angry with him for something he'd said. Probably because he had tried to convince her to apply as principal in a different school district. He knew her well enough to know that she would keep her anger inside until she had to release it.

Matthew tried to conceal his aggravation and sat next to her on the sofa. He touched Autumn's hand. "Tell me what I can do to make it right between us again?"

She turned to face him. "It's too late, Matthew.

What we had before left when you walked out on me. I know that I hurt you, but what I'm just beginning to understand is why I couldn't go to you and tell you that I was ill. Finally, I've figured out why. We've never had the closeness to talk about what was important for me. It was always about you."

"Wait, Autumn."

She held her hands up to stop him. "No, you wait. I could have died the night you left, and you knew that I was hurt. You didn't come to see if I was all right, or call my parents to inquire about my health. I would have if it were you. Don't you know that I would have walked through fire for you?"

"So this is it? I forgive you for what you've done, and now you don't want me?" He was insulted. He had stopped seeing the nurse he was going to marry and gone back to Autumn. Now she was dumping him. "I can't believe you're doing this to us. I forgave you, and now you have the attitude like you're high-quality."

"Matthew, I was a sex addict, and one of your colleagues slept with me, the woman who you were engaged to marry. You finding out must have been devastating. It had to be the worst betrayal to find out that I was sleeping around. I know that I'm damaged goods, you made that clear." She folded her arms and looked away from him. For a moment she remembered how her father had reacted and the betrayal he'd felt when he found out. The secret nearly caused her parents to divorce.

"Yes, you did take me back, but the memory of that night will always be with me. The hatred and disgust you felt toward me was like a knife piercing through my heart. It could never be the same between us and it's my fault."

"But I came back," he interrupted. "Doesn't that mean anything?"

"Yes, it does, but since we were apart it has given me a chance to see what we had, and to see it for what it really was. We are not meant to be together. I know that now. We are too different, Matthew. You have no respect for my career or anything that I want in life. You have no respect for me. Why did you come back?" She was now facing him.

Matthew shook his head in disbelief. "Because I love you."

"But you're not in love with me. Why did you really come back?" she demanded.

"Listen, Autumn, I was engaged to marry another woman and we broke it off. A month ago I realized that I was still in love with you."

"After your engagement was broken you realized that you still loved me? If you really loved me you wouldn't have gotten engaged. From the way it sounds, she probably left you, then you came running back to me on the rebound."

She had hit a raw spot, and he was getting irritated and angry. He wouldn't discuss his relationship with Krista. That was his business and he refused to talk about it.

"Do you realize how lucky you are that I came back after what you did? No man would want you after you cheated, and no man would marry you if he knew what you were," he said maliciously.

Autumn stood up. She was fed up with the conversation, and it was over with her and Matthew, so why prolong it any longer? He needed to grow up, and Betty was right, he was a selfish man.

"I'm not going to thank you for coming back to me for the rest of my life. I think you should leave." She would no longer tolerate his disrespect and pointed at the door. Autumn started to walk away when she felt his grip tighten around her arm.

"I won't be back you know."

"I know."

"You are stupid, Autumn. You always were, and you know that you still love me. All of a sudden you're a principal and now you think you're all that."

"I've always tried to prove myself to you and be a better person because you had me convinced that I wasn't good enough. And you're absolutely right; I was stupid. Looking at you tonight, and listening to you, with all I've done I have finally realized that I am a better person than you are. You're not good enough for me. We are finished. We are through. We are over." She was angry, but relieved. Both hands rested on her hips, her head held high. In Matthew's presence, for the first time she felt confident, powerful, and good about herself. He'd said no man would ever marry her, but she knew one who would. She couldn't marry Matthew when deep inside she was still in love with Philip.

As Matthew stopped at the door, he heard the words that he had used the night he walked out of her life. "We're finished. We're through. We're over." The words hit him in the face like a ton of bricks and he turned to look at her one last time.

Chapter 21

She cleared her desk to go home. Two weeks had passed, and Matthew hadn't called Autumn. But she was relieved. Autumn had settled into her job as principal and was learning how to make her position easier and was becoming better at accomplishing more for the good of the children. The only thing missing in her life was Philip. She had come to realize that Lacy was right. Autumn had broken off her engagement from Philip because it was too hard to look at his face since he knew about her. But he knew they had shared a one-night stand when he first told her that he loved her. He just didn't understand why. So why was she so reluctant to pick up the phone and call the man? She sat at her desk and stared at the phone. Every time she thought of him she wondered if Philip still loved her, but still, she could not will herself to call him.

Autumn knew that she had to get her mind back on the report that she was preparing for the administrator from the Unified School District. He would arrive tomorrow morning.

That evening, Autumn stopped at the Subway to purchase a turkey sandwich on the way home. Once she got home, she changed into a bathrobe and took a Pepsi from the refrigerator. She grabbed the newspaper and sat at the kitchen counter, placing her sandwich in front of her. She sighed and looked at the phone, then the clock. If she called Philip now, she could still reach him before he left his job. With trembling hands, Autumn dialed the number and listened while the phone rang. To her disappointment, the call went straight to his voicemail and she hung up without leaving a message. She closed her eyes, feeling frustrated. It had taken her all day to muster enough nerve to call him. Finally, she did and got his voicemail. "Why am I so stupid," she asked herself out loud. The doorbell rang and she started not to answer. It rang again and irritated her with the disruption so she leaped from the counter and walked to the door.

Autumn opened the door and stood breathlessly as she stared up at him. Her heartbeat quickened and her legs weakened. Seeing him smile made it hard for her to stand.

"May I come in?" Philip asked.

"Of course you can." Autumn moved aside as he brushed past her.

She sat on the sofa, and Philip sat beside her. They started to speak at the same time.

Autumn cleared her throat. "I'll go first. The night I found out that you remembered me, I was angry because you had kept it a secret. But I was mostly angry and ashamed of myself. I wanted to be the proper, pure wife, and I wanted you to always have the utmost respect for me."

"Okay. Now it's my turn." He took her hand in his.

"I have more respect for you than for anyone I know. And yes, I should have told you. But Autumn, we got along so well together and I had fallen in love with you. I didn't want to spoil anything for us, and I didn't want our relationship to change. Do you think that you can ever forgive me?"

Autumn smiled. "I already have. I just called your office before you arrived."

"Will you marry me?"

Her eyes lit up, and a smile pulled at the corners of her mouth. "Yes. I'd love to marry you. I've missed you so much, Philip." He pulled her into his arms and kissed her.

"Do you have to go home tonight?" she asked and snuggled her face into his neck.

"I won't go home tonight. Anyway, I drove by the house that we wanted to buy, and the realtor was there. She let me borrow the key. Why don't we go and take another look at it?"

"I can't believe such a beautiful house is still for sale." Autumn looked excited. "Could we really be so lucky?"

"Some things are meant for people, just as we're meant for each other, baby."

Autumn rushed into her bedroom. She slipped into her jeans and oversized T-shirt, applied lipstick, and strode brusquely back to the living room with her purse swinging on her arm.

Philip stood up and kissed her. "I missed seeing your smile. It always lights up my heart."

"I missed you more."

Hand in hand they walked to his car. While Philip drove, Autumn told him about her promotion to principal. She looked at his face; he was proud of her work. Telling Philip was so different from telling Matthew.

Philip parked the car in the driveway and opened the door for Autumn.

"It was nice of the realtor to lend you the key until tomorrow. But if it were me, I would have done the same for you. You must melt the womens' hearts," she said jokingly.

"I only want to melt your heart, dear. But she couldn't help herself," Philip said smiling. He looked down the quiet street.

They stepped inside the house, and Philip switched on a lamp as Autumn stood in the living room. She started toward the kitchen that she'd fallen in love with the first time, but with no explanation something kept her in the familiar living room. She stood there for a while, then went and peeked in all the rooms as though she wasn't sure if they were changed. Were they larger, smaller?

"Do you still like the house, Autumn?" Philip followed her from room to room.

"Do I ever. I love it even more than before. But the furniture arrangement seems to be different. I wonder why. Maybe the seller wants the house to look larger, or give it a different appeal, but I don't understand why.

"Really?" Philip asked, and followed her to the bedroom.

Autumn stopped at the bedroom door with a frown. "I love it. Don't you?" She was completely taken aback.

Philip followed her back to the living room, and Autumn looked at the fireplace. Her eyes shot up, and her brows met suspiciously over the middle of them. She went closer to the fireplace and saw the picture of her and Philip that was taken when they went exploring at Venice Beach. She looked at the furniture again, then at Philip.

Philip couldn't contain himself any longer and laughed out loud. "I bought the house and moved into it. I knew how much you loved it. This was the house that we had planned to raise our children in."

Autumn felt a lump in her throat as she looked at him, her eyes glowing with love. She fell into his arms and promised herself that she would never leave this man again. He meant the world to her. She was speechless and had never felt so loved, so wanted, or so much in love. "What did I do to deserve you, and all you know about me, Philip?"

"You're my life, Autumn." His eyes were smoldering with passion for her. She had never experienced such intense, trembling anticipation for a man's body. Not even when she was ill and needed it most. With Philip it was different. She wanted to make love, not just for the sex, but for the man whom she loved and wanted to make happy.

"Let's go to our bedroom, baby." He took her hand and led her to the bed. It would be the first night in their new house together.

Philip made love to her slowly. He wanted everything at once, to touch her, look at her, and taste her.

As always, Philip surprised her with his gentle and skillful hands. All of a sudden, both of them climaxed violently. Then, completely sated and their legs entwined, he gathered her into his arms. They lay still gasping for air.

Finally, Autumn sat up and rested on one elbow.

"We are in our house. I thought that we had lost it." She snuggled against him. "Philip?"

"Yes, love?"

"I don't want you to worry about my sex addiction. When we broke up, the only urges I had were for you. I haven't had sex with anyone since you." She couldn't even have sex with Matthew, she just couldn't. Now she realized that deep inside her head, it would have been cheating on Philip. She hadn't realized it until now that she had no sex urges for Matthew, at least not enough to sleep with him.

With both hands, Philip cupped Autumn's face. "I'm not worried about you at all. I know what kind of woman you are inside, and I know that you love me. We're comfortable and at peace when we are together, and our marriage will be solid. But baby, please stay addicted to having sex with me," Philip said teasing her devilishly.

Autumn laughed. "Oh, but I intend to."

They stayed awake late and planned their wedding. Both lay on their sides, resting on their elbows.

"You can move in when you are ready. I need you here with me."

"I'll start packing on the weekend. But what about my furniture?" she asked. She had only bought her bedroom furniture a year ago.

"We can compromise and you don't have to get rid of anything. All you have to do is marry me, love me and we will be happy, forever."

"I love you so much now, and at last we will be happy, forever," Autumn whispered.

Look For These Other
Dafina Novels